The Witch of Rollright

MERLIN PRICE

First published by Rex Collings Ltd 1979

To Giovanna

One

The blue double-decker bus churned the mud against the hedges as it engaged low gear and began the pull up Long Compton Hill. Its cargo of excited children from Roddwych Middle School gazed across the fields. In bottom gear the ancient bus swerved across the main Oxford road and chugged along towards the Rollright Stones.

It trundled to a halt in the lay-by and its doors opened. The children crowded off, clutching work-sheets and clip boards and assembled near the gate-way to the field. They chattered noisily as two teachers counted them and herded them to a gate which bore the sign 'NO ENTRY BETWEEN SUNSET AND SUNRISE'.

The wind gusted through them and there was the usual outcry against the weather, lapsing into quiet giggles as Mr Taylor, the headteacher, strode forward in ancient wellingtons and torn anorak. He slipped the catch on the gate and the children surged through and spread out thinly amongst the stones. Eager figures paced the Circle and muttered counting filled the air.

'I've lost count!'

'Well, how many did you get it to?'

Pinched red faces and frosty breath as cold hands scribbled interesting details.

'I bet them girls didn't fancy dancin' with no clothes on in this weather!'

'Oh shut up Simon! Here, look at the holes in this one!'

Pieces of paper ruffled in the gusts. Poems were begun. A tractor clattered across a nearby field. Mr Taylor waved his arms frantically as Simon and John clambered up one of the stones.

'Can't you boys read?'

They slid down again, sheepish, until his eyes were off them and then renewed their attempt on its summit.

'Look at all these little holes!'

'It says its "oolitic limestone" in our handout,' said one of the girls knowledgeably.

'Who-licked-it limestone,' said Simon and gave the girl a push. The wind caught her papers and pulled them from the clip. They fanned across the centre of the circle.

'You sod!'

She ran after them, treading on the last one and leaving a perfect imprint of her foot on it in brown mud.

'Now look what you've done!'

Simon grinned at her. It was great, a day off, just look at that tractor! The girl left him and wandered away.

Across the road a single finger of rock, larger than all the other stones, seemed to beckon her. She wrinkled up her muddied paper and shoved it into her pocket. She headed towards Mr Barnes who was explaining one of the stories connected with the stones.

'It's a megalithic circle, over a hundred feet in diameter.'

'How did the stones get here, Mr Barnes?'

'No one knows for certain, but they do say that no one can count them and get the same answer twice. By the way, if you look carefully you'll find that the lanes all around the hill-top meet here. Perhaps it was an ancient gathering place or a temple to the sun. As I said, no one really knows how or when these stones first appeared.'

'What's that over there?' asked the girl who had lost her papers. Everyone turned to look at the single stone across the road.

'That's the Kingstone, Sarah,' replied Mr Barnes. 'If you read your notes you'll find the story about it. It's said that a Pagan King heard tell that if he and his Knights climbed the hill until they could see Long Compton village then the crown of England would be his. There's an old rhyme:

"When Long Compton you shall see
You shall King of England be."'

'What happened?' asked Sarah.

'Well, this witch from the village stopped the King in his tracks, so the story goes, and said:

"As Long Compton thou canst not see
King of England thou shalt not be.
Rise up stick and stand thou stone
For King of England thou shalt be none

Thou and thy men hoar stones shall be
And I myself an eldern tree."

The King was turned into what's now called the Kingstone and his Knights became those stones over there.'

Mr Barnes pointed to where the tractor was churning across the field. A clump of rock stood out clearly through the crowd of the birds that followed the plough.

'The rest of his army is this stone circle here.'

'So these stones were supposed to have been real people?' asked Sarah.

'Yes, some people say that if you pierce them with a knife they bleed.'

The group of children broke up and Simon took out his pen-knife.

'Watch they don't turn on you,' laughed John.

Simon scraped his knife against the stone.

'Bloody hell!'

Blood gushed out of his finger where the knife had slipped.

'Oh! Come and look Mr Barnes! Simon's made it bleed!'

Simon wrapped his finger in his handkerchief and grinned sheepishly.

'Sorry Mr Barnes, me hand slipped.'

Sarah wandered down towards the road and John walked across to join her. Although they were brother and sister they were very different from one another. John was basically happy-go-lucky, never letting anything worry him for too long, whereas Sarah, standing on the verge of adolescence, almost a year older than her brother, had always tended to be rather quiet and serious. Lately she had come to treat John and his circle of friends with a certain degree of aloofness. Their mother had died a few years before and they had been brought up by their father, who ran a small bakery in Roddwych. Nevertheless, whilst John shook his head in mock exasperation at Sarah's incipient womanliness, a strong bond still held them together, although she was less inclined than ever to join in with his somewhat extrovert activities.

'Do you reckon they'll let us go over to look at the Kingstone?' Sarah asked.

'Come on, let's go ourselves,' replied John. He lifted the catch and they stepped into the road. The bus stood waiting, the driver engrossed in his newspaper.

They clambered over the stile on the other side of the road and along the muddy pathway that curved towards the Kingstone.

'Pity it's covered by railings,' said John, as he side-stepped a large cow-pat.

Sarah walked around the stone.

'You can see a face in it!' she gasped.

'You're imagining things again!' declared John. Sarah's over-active imagination had been a matter of dispute between them for some months now. On several occasions she had made an issue over her 'feelings' towards certain places and things, sometimes even refusing to stay in a particular room if it didn't feel right. John put it down to the changes she was going through, together with her long silences and occasional outbreaks of bad temper.

Sarah glared at him, and seeing that he had overstepped the mark he tried to pacify her. 'Mind you, that craggy bit does look very much like Mr Taylor!'

Sarah laughed.

'Perhaps you're right. I probably was imagining things.'

She sorted through her work-sheets.

'It says here that someone once tried to move the Kingstone a couple of hundred years ago.'

'Pickfords,' laughed John.

'Don't be daft. Mr Barnes wouldn't have put it down if it wasn't true.'

'What happened?'

'Oh, they got it half-way down the hill and then they had to take it back again.'

'Sounds like the Grand Old Duke of York! Why did they take it back?'

'No idea.'

'What on earth did they want it for in the first place?'

'Bridging a stream, I think.'

'I bet it was a weight. Hey up! There's Mr Barnes trying to round everyone up.'

'Let's just have one more look.'

'Come on, you know what he's like if you wander off. "Letting the school down again. Won't be allowed on any more trips."'

They scurried across to the stile. Sarah balanced on the cross bar.

'You know,' she said to herself, 'I'm sure if you look hard enough you can see a face.'

The knot of children stood around their teachers and, as Sarah and John approached, the group began to break up and head towards the road.

'Have you been across to see the Kingstone already?' asked Mr Taylor.

'Yes,' replied Sarah, 'it's gigantic, and I'm certain you can see a face in it if you look closely enough.'

Mr Taylor laughed.

'Wait here if you like, as you've already been to have a look. We'll be back in a couple of minutes or so, then we'll have to be heading back.'

The noise from the rest of the class died away as they clambered over the stile and reappeared near the Kingstone.

'That King almost made it,' said John. 'It's only about two more steps before you can see the village from over there.'

'I wonder what happened to the witch?' said Sarah. 'It says in the rhyme that she was turned into an eldern tree. I suppose that's what we'd call an elder nowadays. Hey! There's a man in that hut. Kathryn told me she got some post-cards off him. I think I'll go and have a look.'

'I'm going to count the stones again.' said John, and set off counting slowly and deliberately. He reached 37 before his voice faded into the distance.

Sarah headed towards the hut.

It stood on one side of the circle, nestling in the small cluster of trees. It looked as if it belonged in the story of Hansel and Gretel, thought Sarah. She wondered if the man lived there all the time. Perhaps it even had its own toilet. She smiled to herself. It would be a bit cold if you had to go outside, particularly in the winter.

The hut had a kind of stable door, with a top and bottom on separate hinges. Leaning over the lower part was a man. He was young and had long flowing hair and a beard. Around his neck he wore a Celtic cross. Sarah shivered. He could almost be one of the Knights!

'Hello.'

'Hello,' his eyes twinkled, and Sarah smiled.

'What happened to the witch?'

The young man smiled again.

'She was turned into a tree.'

'Which one?' Sarah glanced around.

'Oh, they cut it down years ago, but rumour has it that it stood near the blackthorn bush over the road near the Kingstone.'

'I thought it might have still been there.'

'No love, just the stones are here now, though some would argue about that!'

'How do you mean?'

'Well they say no man living has counted them and got the same figure twice running. I've counted them myself and always got a different number.'

'How many are there supposed to be?'

'Some say 70, others 77. I've counted 75 and 74 at times.'

'I suppose it's hard to count with some lying on the ground and half hidden?'

'You'd think so, but when you go around they all seem clear enough at the time. It's when you arrive back that you find it adds up wrong.'

'77!'

John stepped up behind Sarah and placed his cold fingers on her neck.

'Beware the Stone King's Hand!'

'There you are!' said the young man. 'Your friend seems to have got it right!'

'Clever-clogs!' said Sarah, and after buying a postcard strolled back towards the road. Already the rest of the group were making their way back towards the bus. Mr Taylor and Mr Barnes shepherded them aboard, and after a final count of heads, the engine started up and the old double-decker turned and headed ponderously towards Roddwych and school.

Two

The bus arrived back at the school. It was already dark and Sarah stood aside as the crowd pushed into the cloakroom area. John grabbed for his coat and barged towards the door.

'Fancy being up at the Stones now?' he asked Sarah as he passed.

'Not likely, but I wish we'd had more time to look at them. Oh! I'll have to finish this poem at home, I'd forgotten I'd got mud all over my first copy.'

'How about us biking up there on Saturday?' suggested John suddenly. He knew that lately Sarah had felt that she should spend most of the weekend doing house-work and helping her father make up orders in the shop, yet it had been a long time since they had been out for the day together, and he felt he needed to get to know the new person that was gradually emerging from the child that used to be his sister.

'You know Dad needs help on Saturdays in the shop.'

'I'm sure he wouldn't mind, just this once, we haven't been out for a ride for ages.'

Sarah put on her coat and picked up her clip-board. She stepped around the other children who were noisily trying to collect their coats and bags.

'I'll see what Dad says.'

'Oh I'm sure he'll let us go!' John said.

'Go where?'

Simon appeared, his blue duffle-coat pulled awkwardly on and his usual happy grin firmly in place. Simon was John's best friend. He tended to worship Sarah from afar, and was more than a little in awe of her. Sarah didn't think he was very bright.

'Up to the Rollright Stones tomorrow,' replied John. 'Do you fancy coming?'

Sarah groaned inwardly. Simon's acceptance of the offer however was not immediately forthcoming. He seemed a little ruffled.

'You didn't ought to spend too much time up there, least that's what my old man says,' he said slowly. 'He says funny things happen around

Long Compton. In fact he wasn't too keen on me coming with the school today.'

'Scared of the bogey-men?' asked Sarah.

Simon reddened.

'Nah,' he glanced at John for support. 'It's just me Dad didn't think it were a good place. I weren't scared!'

'The bogey-man made you cut your finger,' teased Sarah. Simon unwound his handkerchief which he still had wrapped around his hand.

'Tain't nothing,' he replied. His face brightened.

'Yeah! I'll come!'

'Are you sure your Dad will let you?' inquired Sarah solicitously.

John ended the matter.

'If you can come, we'll meet you at the Post Office at the end of our street at 12 o'clock. If you aren't there by ten past, we'll go on.'

'See you then,' said Simon.

They hurried out of school.

'Why on earth did you ask your idiot friend along?'

'Oh! He's all right. You aren't half critical!'

The welcoming yellow glow of the school faded and their footsteps echoed across the playground and into the frosty evening.

The next morning was Saturday. It was cold and there was a touch of frost. Sarah had been up since eight o'clock and, having made breakfast, washed up, and helped out in the shop, she had waited for John to return from delivering the orders. When he arrived back she popped her head into the shop where her father was counting up the bread orders for the week.

'John and I are going for a ride to Long Compton,' she called. 'You don't mind do you?'

'You take care to be back by tea-time,' replied her father. 'You'd best take some of these fancies with you.' He picked out four pastries, still warm from the night's baking. He placed them in a greaseproof bag and handed them to her. 'There's some cheese-cake in the fridge cabinet, if you've a mind to take it as well.'

'Thanks, Dad!'

Sarah was out of the door before he could reply.

'Is it OK?' John's face peered anxiously into the kitchen.

'Yes, come on, but we've got to be back for tea.'

'Great!'

'Dad gave us some pastries to take with us. If we get a couple of bags of crisps from the Post Office that should be enough.'

They wheeled their bikes down to the corner shop and Sarah disappeared inside to buy some crisps.

'There's no sign of Simon.' said John, looking at his watch.

'Probably afraid of the bogey-man,' replied Sarah. 'Come on, it's ten past already.'

'Let's just hang on a minute,' said John.

At that moment Simon appeared cycling hurriedly around the corner. He waved, wobbled, corrected his course and swerved towards them.

'Hi! Told you I'd be here!'

'You're late,' announced Sarah coldly.

'Had to help me Gran – went to the supermarket. Here, I got these!'

He held up three packets of crisps.

'Oh great!' enthused Sarah. 'That's just what we wanted, what a varied diet!' She held up the packets she had bought in the Post Office. 'They're not even cheese and onion flavour.' she added in a disgusted tone.

'Oh, come on,' said John. 'We're wasting time.'

He pedalled off, leaving Sarah and Simon to stuff the offending packets into their saddle-bags. The roads were clear, with only the occasional car passing them, and the journey across the countryside was enjoyable, with the faint tang of mist on their lips. The wheels of the bicycles made crisp, crunching noises as they passed over the layer of frost and dead leaves that lay at the edge of the road. They were soon coasting through Shipston and along the road to Long Compton.

'Shall we go straight up to the Stones or look around the village first?' Sarah panted.

'Let's go up to the Stones. It'll be dark before we have chance to have a good look around otherwise.' replied John. 'We can go and look in the village afterwards.'

Simon looked up.

'Reckon I'll get a bottle of pop from the village shop,' he said.

'Good idea.'

They soon came to the village and cycled past the Church and the large houses that lined the main road. On their right stood the village stores, and John and Sarah rested briefly while Simon went in to buy a drink. He came out a few minutes later with a large bottle of lemonade.

'We'll be glad of this at the top of the hill.'

They remounted their bikes and pedalled on. The slope began to pull at their leg muscles. They passed the 'Red Lion' on their right.

'If my Dad were here he'd be in there for a pint,' said Simon conversationally. 'He's a great one for the beer is my Dad.'

Sarah pursed her lips. John smiled.

They lapsed into silence as they rounded the bend at the foot of the hill, reserving their breath for the effort of climbing upwards. Half-way Sarah stopped and rolled her bike into the ditch.

'Oh, let's have a quick rest. Here Simon, give us a swig of your lemonade.'

Simon meekly removed the bottle from his saddle-bag and handed it to her.

'Ahh! That's better.' She handed it back to Simon.

'Want some?' He offered the bottle to John.

'Thanks.' John drank gratefully.

Simon stoppered the bottle and put it away.

They lifted their bikes from the roadside and pushed them up the remainder of the hill. The mists still clung to the lower levels of the village, but up towards the Stones the sky was clearing and the day was cold and sharp. The hedgerows were silent, and apart from the occasional car whispering by, the air was still.

As they reached the right-hand fork that led towards the Stones they heard the sound of the tractor that they had seen the previous day. They cycled the few hundred yards to the lay-by and, resting their bikes against the fence near the gateway, they wandered inside.

There were one or two people already strolling around inside the circle.

'It looks different when you're on our own,' said Sarah. 'More scary.'

John had set off around the stones.

'He's not counting them again is he?' groaned Sarah.

'I ain't half hungry,' said Simon, his mind more on the crisps in his saddlebag than the Stones. 'Let's go and have the food we brought.'

Sarah glanced at her watch. It was twenty minutes to three. She realised that she too felt hungry and that lunch was rather overdue. They turned to look for John who had now reached the far side of the circle.

'Yoohoo!'

John looked up briefly and in a manner that indicated that he had more important things to concentrate on than food. Simon headed towards his bike and having removed his crisps and lemonade he squatted down on the grass verge and opened one of the packets. Sarah took out the pastries that she had brought.

'There's four here,' she said. 'That's one each and we'll keep one for whoever's hungriest on the way back.'

Simon's eyes lit up. He took the pastry from Sarah and wolfed it down. Sarah looked at him carefully.

'Are you that hungry?'

'Well, I didn't have no breakfast. Me Dad had to go out and me Mam was round at Gran's.'

'You'd best have the other one as well.'

'No, it's all right.' Simon realised he'd made a fool of himself. 'Save it for John,' he grinned a little shamefacedly. 'I bet he'll get it down him fast enough!'

They looked over the fencing. To their surprise, John was embarking on a second circuit of the Stones.

'Oi!' they shouted, 'Dinner is served!'

John didn't even lift his head. His finger was moving, pointing at each stone in turn. He continued around the circle without looking to right or left.

'He looks like one of them toy trains you get at the fair,' laughed Simon. 'Hey John, hurry up and get to a station or I'll eat yer pastry!'

But John was now on the far side and lost to hearing.

A middle-aged man accompanied by an older woman appeared at the gate. The man glanced idly at the two children enjoying their make-shift meal on the grass verge. He hurried to a large car that stood parked in the lay-by. The old woman paused as she walked past them.

'Didn't you see the sign?' she snarled. 'No picnics!'

Sarah glanced up in surprise. Simon butted in.

'But that means inside, not outside,' he said.

'Makes no difference, inside or out, you're not supposed to sit around here. You've seen the Stones, so there's no need to lounge about leaving litter.'

'We're waiting for our friend,' said Simon and pointed to the distant figure of John, now scarcely visible behind the larger stones.

The woman snorted and with a further backward glance stamped off to the car.

Simon grinned. He turned to Sarah.

'Bit lah-di-dah weren't she?' he commented.

Sarah's face had turned white. She dug her fingernails into her palms in an effort to control a feeling of panic that welled up inside her.

'That woman......' she began.

'Sarah! Simon!'

'What is it?' called Simon.

They turned to see John scrambling through the gate. Encumbered by his anorak he was having difficulty in struggling between the gate-posts.

'I've just counted the Stones!'

'Congratulations!' exclaimed Simon. 'I'll tell Mr Barnes on Monday. He'll be sure to give you an extra star in Maths!'

'No, you stupid sod!' gasped John. 'You see I counted them yesterday and there's one missing!'

Sarah and Simon looked at him. Sarah had never seen him look this serious. She was the first to speak, all thoughts of the woman and the strange feeling that had engulfed her set aside.

'But you know the legend! It's like the man said. He'd never got the same number twice. You've just made a mistake in the counting, that's all.'

'No, I've counted them twice. There's one missing!'

'Oh, get away, look, how many were there yesterday?'

'77.'

'And how many are there now?'

'76!'

'Well, you're only one out! That's not bad, even the man that's here all the time was further out than that!'

'I tell you there's one missing.' John was almost in tears.

'How can you be so sure?'

'Because I know which one it is!'

There was a silence.

'You see, yesterday, as part of our project work, I did a sketch of a group of four or five of the stones in the circle, and it's one of them that's disappeared!'

'Oh you probably made a mistake in your drawing.'

'Come and look then!'

John had dragged a rumpled drawing out of his pocket.

'I made a rough copy first, and shoved it in my jacket. Here it is! Now look. This is where I did my drawing. See the other stones? They're the

15

same, aren't they? But that one. It's not there anymore, and there's no sign of it anywhere nearby. I tell you one of the stones has gone.'

Three

The white mists had already eaten away the lakeside when the old man stumbled into the camp. His clothing was stained with mud and dirt and his bare feet were blackened. The soldiers had dealt roughly with him at the guard post for this was a time of suspicion, when even kinsmen were to be distrusted. Yet he carried himself well, more like a noble than a captured serf. His wild statements held enough truth for the guard to call the master-at-arms. Eventually the King himself, sleepless and troubled after the ritual at the lakeside, questioned him and heard his prophecy, before the blood welled into the old man's throat and his body was consigned to the dark waters of the lake.

Sunlight dissolved the mist as the victorious army roused up and pressed on towards its goal. Fires were damped, and the soldiers, wet and hungry, struggled through the clinging mud whilst the Knights rode forward. At their head, the King, resplendent on a white horse, listened to the chill wind as it whispered to him the words of the old man.

Before dawn the next day the army halted and the King slowly dismounted. The soldiers waited, muttering to themselves. And as they waited wild rumour ran amongst them. The old man at the last camp. What news had he brought? The King himself had been summoned!

Some said that he had sought to bargain, others that he had been a warlock who had dared to threaten the king. The Knights who had stood in council knew better.

All night the King had consulted with them and, as the old man had gurgled away his life, his throat neatly severed by the master-at-arms, they had been convinced of his strange prediction.

'When Long Compton you shall see
You shall King of England be'

The fingers of dawn slid between the larch trees and into the clearing. The King stood silhouetted against the headland. Below lay the village of Long Compton.

He beckoned his Knights to move aside. The Gods had spoken, the gift at the lake had been accepted. He strode out of the sun and up towards the crest of the hill to meet his destiny.

The hideous rags that lay against the blackthorn bush turned as his night-cloak rustled past. The sun reached the tree tops and the mist rolled down Long Compton Hill and into the village. Sunlight gleamed yellow on the giant stones that were all that remained of the army that had clustered together a moment ago in the clearing.

Up on the headland a mighty stone stood, alone, facing into the wind, bent with a timeless weight of frustrated rage.

The man had become lame during the long march of the past two days. Now he sought the camp, his mouth dry with fear, for he well knew the penalty for desertion. But what use could he be in battle? A humble mason knew none of the arts of a fighting man. Still, he would be glad to find them again. In this weather a night without fire was to court the attentions of witches and evil spirits.

He found his King, and the army too, but it turned his senses, for he had many friends amongst those ghastly stones that now stood in silence. Yet his mind was cunning, and soon he realised that he alone was living witness to the Act of Appeasement of two nights past. Taking his tools he ventured to the single stone. Delicately he sought a place upon its surface hidden from the gaze of fools and swiftly set about his work.

Now he must lie low, for it was clear that strange powers were held by those who dwelt in the village at the foot of the hill.

They found him a few hours later, raving of stones and hidden markings, and of great riches. But despite all their foul means of persuasion he revealed nothing that made sense, and he died suddenly, late that night. They placed his bones beyond Long Compton Church.

******

'God damn and blast your eyes Hugh Boffin!' A swarthy thickset man struggled at the reins as the team of horses bucked and rolled their eyes, the sweat steaming out into the autumn morning. Henry Jeffs wished that he'd stayed at home rather than help his neighbour in such a foolish scheme. The stone lay brown and yellow on the road, bound tight and harnessed to the team. Its passage had gouged a scar along the track and the horses were now in such a lather that it seemed it must be rooted to the ground.

Only the previous night Hugh had mentioned in the village inn that he'd found the very thing to bridge the culvert that ran by his house. Everyone knew those stones could not be counted.

'Then who would miss the one?' he'd argued. Tongues had wagged at this and many of the old stories were retold concerning the stone circle. Young Henry had been glad of company on his way home that night. Of course the tales of witches in the village were common knowledge. Hadn't Harry Sheldon told of the midsummer night he'd visited the stones in search of naked girls doing their dance to foretell their future husbands? Harry had caught cold from his night's adventure and carried flannel in is boots for a month.

'There's enough witches in Long Compton to draw a wagon-load of hay up Long Compton Hill.' That's what his father always said.

He was glad to get past the Churchyard. Outside its door lay an effigy in stone. Henry knew this to be of Saint Augustine, and there was a tale about that too, and of a dead man forced to walk again. But best not to think of it at this time of night!

So here he was next morning, trying to control these skittish nags. Steam poured from their nostrils and their whinnies echoed down the hill. Hugh Boffin cursed and flung his arms around the lead horse's neck. It broke away and the team careered against each other, pulling the stone into the verge. Henry looked at the stone more carefully. It was gigantic, for much of it had been buried in the ground. He could see the darkened part that had lain beneath the soil.

Hugh Boffin wiped his neck with a scrap of rag and glared at the stone.

'It's as how it don't want to come,' he muttered, and turning to look down the hill he cursed again and began to unhitch the horses.

'I reckon it'd better go back.'

Henry marched the lead horse to the stone and re-harnessed it. As Hugh brought up the rest of the team the lead horse cried out. Muscles heaving and head pulled back with fear, it reared and scrambled up the hill. The giant stone strained against the harness and slowly moved. Gradually it slid from out of the ditch. Gaining speed the horse cantered up the hill trailing the stone behind it. When Hugh and Henry caught up, the horse was grazing near the circle and the stone lay silent on the headland from where its journey had begun.

'Begod if that horse 'asn't got the strength of six,' said Hugh Boffin proudly. 'But maybe that stone had best stay here a while longer. I'll find some wood that'll take its place over my culvert.' He led the team away and Henry Jeffs turned to look at the wind-aged giant. It gleamed in the strengthening light. Across the track the Rollright Circle held silence as the stepping hooves of Boffin's horses died away.

'The horse has not been reared that can pull nigh on three ton of rock,' muttered Henry to himself. But he resolved to keep this strange occurrence secret, at least for the time being. As the years passed however he related the events of that day, and whilst his children and grand-children found it a fine enough tale, his friends at the 'Red Lion' were rather more sceptical.

****

The wind howled across the fields and around the figure that shouted and wrestled vainly with a pitchfork. The stalks were blowing across the hedges and the angry sky brushed the clouds in the direction of the Hill. The figure abandoned its struggle and ran across the field to the gateway. Halting for a moment, it turned, retrieved the pitchfork, and with a purposeful stride, stepped down the Hill and into the village.

In Clark's Lane, Nanny Shipton was making towards the door of her neat little cottage, a freshly bought loaf in her hand. Eighty years old she was, with the lined handsome face of a woman who for years had been close to the weather. People in the village were a little afraid of her. The stories of witchcraft died hard, and people still remembered the tales of a hundred years ago when old Henry Jeffs had been put under an evil eye by Mary Shipton. If it hadn't been for John Wheeler the schoolmaster he would have died, they said. John Wheeler had taken his own nail-parings and burned them in the oven, this being a known cure for a witch's curse. As soon as they began to burn, Mary Shipton's screams had echoed all through the village.

Old Nanny Shipton lifted her head to the wind. It blew from over the hill-top, and ears of corn whipped in it, gathered from the surrounding fields. There was the scent of approaching autumn, and the sky threatened rain. That tense feeling that comes with blustery weather held the village in its grip and there was tell of cattle sickening and horses dead.

From the corner of her eye Nanny Shipton saw his face. By then the pitchfork had done its work and Master Woodward's arm, strengthened from his labours, brought a swift end. The bloodied rags lay crumpled at the cottage door and her only cry summoned neighbours who bore away the crazed farmer's lad.

The trial was brief and Master Woodward exclaimed that Nanny Shipton had deserved her fate, and sixteen other hags in the village too. He had been bewitched and could not work. The water he had drunk had been cursed.

'Let her body be weighed against the Church Bible,' he had cried out in court.

The jury returned a verdict of 'Not Guilty but insane' and the Judge pronounced that something should be done to disabuse the minds of the village people of a belief in witch-craft in this year of enlightenment Eighteen hundred and Seventy-five.

Master Woodward died a few months later in Warwick jail.

The news drew scant attention.

The winds of winter howled over the headland and the stone figures above the village brooded on.

Four

The heavy velvet curtains were drawn across the windows although it was still afternoon and outside the sun shone faintly through the gathering clouds. A thin ray of sunlight made specks of dust dance through the narrow gap, until a gin-white hand with painted nails twitched it closed. The sunlight ended and the dust settled.

A smell of rotting things and rooms unused to light. The Watchers stood silent beside an old table made of elder-wood. No light save that given by a solitary candle in the darkness. A moan arose, lifted, swept higher, and was gone.

Words.

Words no longer spoken, no longer written.

Old Words.

Words of Power and Strength.

For a moment the stillness of the room became absolute, as if time had stopped. Outside, the sounds of the village faded. The candle grew dim. Flared up. Died.

'It does not come.'

She spoke.

'The time is not right. The Power is not yet with the Words. Or else the Lore has changed! Yet I feel the shadow of the Power. It must be right. The time is soon, and our work will be rewarded.'

The hand reached out again, and waning sunlight blanched the room. The hum of the traffic on the main road filtered in once more and vibrated the latches of the heavy wooden door. The Watchers filed out and the door closed behind them.

The painted finger-nails tapped against the surface of the elder-wood. The dust renewed its dance before the sunlight faded. As the sun finally died, its last rays lit up the table for a moment, and an age-worn stone gleamed briefly.

The Watchers left the cottage and made their way down Clark's Lane towards the road.

Three children on bicycles hurried by.

She turned from the table.

'The time has almost come.' She spoke in the lowest whisper, as she moved back towards the stone. 'And yet I feel troubled.'

Her fingers rubbed along the edge of the stone, its rough surface encrusted with moss and rusty lichen.

'Things are no longer the same.'

The stone seemed to warm to her touch.

'But I will give you life my friend, and then they all shall see!'

She moved away and the stone grew cold.

Five

Sarah arrived early at school on Monday morning. One or two teachers had already parked their cars and were struggling against the wind with arms full of exercise books and papers. Sarah held open the door for them as they hurried inside.

'Morning, Mrs Gaskill. Morning, Mrs Wright!'

She walked through the foyer and into the Hall. Each morning she was responsible for writing up the titles of hymns for morning assembly on the blackboard. This morning she had an extra reason for wanting to be inside before the others. She wanted to have a word with Mr Barnes about the discovery, and she really didn't want Simon or John to be there overdoing the drama and making it all seem ridiculous.

It was twenty minutes to nine. The doors to the hall opened and Mr Barnes ambled in.

'Good morning, Mr Barnes!'

'Good morning, Sarah. You're bright and early this morning!' He paused only briefly, his mind already working on the possibilities of finding who was responsible for taking the soap from the boys' toilets.

'Mr Barnes!'

Something in the tone of her voice made him turn.

'Yes Sarah? Is anything the matter?'

'Er, well, you know the work we've been doing on the Rollright Stones?'

He nodded.

'I know it sounds daft, but I was up there on Saturday with my brother and Simon.'

'I hope you told your father you were going there. It's a lonely spot.'

'Er, yes, well, anyway, when we went up there with you on Friday John did a drawing of some of the stones, and he tried counting them.

He got the number to 77, but when we got there on Saturday he counted them again and...'

The muted noises of children could be heard through the glass doors of the Hall. Mr Barnes' attention became distracted and, only half listening, he began to move away.

'I'm pleased you took an interest, going up there in your own time.'

'But what I meant to tell you is that one of the stones...'

'Michael! Stuart! Don't push! Hurry up! The bell's gone!'

Mr Barnes stepped through the doors and into the fray.

Sarah snapped the chalk in her fingers.

School began.

'... and when you've finished that piece of work we'll get on with our Project.'

Mr Barnes stepped back from the board and moved across to help a group of children on the far side of the open area. It was a modern school and Sarah's class was one of four whose 'home bay' opened into a wider part furnished with more chairs and tables where the children could work.

'Now's your chance to tell him.' Simon whispered to John who was quickly trying to complete his Maths work.

'In front of the whole class? You're kidding!' replied John. 'And get laughed at by Stuart and his mob? No, we'll keep quiet about it. It's a secret for the time being.'

'...I hear that Sarah, John and Simon have been doing a little more research into the mysteries of the Rollright Stones.'

Mr Barnes was addressing the rest of the class, most of whom had now completed their work.

'Sod it! That's let the cat out of the bag!' groaned John. 'Trust Sarah to go and tell him!'

'And what did you find up there, John?' Mr Barnes asked with interest.

'Not much, Mr Barnes. It was rather spooky so we didn't stay long.'

'Scared of ghosts and goblins?' muttered Stuart Crawford, arch-enemy of John, and ever eager to receive fresh ammunition.

John turned around heatedly.

'Not as much as you'd be, you big ponce!'

'What was that, John?'

'Nothing, Mr Barnes.'

'Mr Barnes,' Sarah had chipped in. 'I was trying to tell you this morning. John counted them again on Saturday and there was one missing!'

'He couldn't count his own fingers!' retorted Stuart.

This gem convulsed the class long enough for Sarah to blush with discomfort, and for John to offer several interesting varieties of violence against the person of Stuart Crawford at break-time.

'I expect you were just mistaken, John,' said Mr Barnes in conciliatory tones.

'No!' burst out Sarah, eager to put the record straight.

'You see he made a sketch!'

'Leave it!' hissed John, wanting nothing more than the whole stupid business to be forgotten.

'... and it was one of the stones that he'd sketched that had disappeared,' continued Sarah. 'At first it didn't look as if anything had been moved, but when we looked more closely you could see that a fresh piece of turf had been placed over the spot where the stone had been.'

The class fell into silence as these new facts were digested.

'How many did you count, John?' asked Mr Barnes.

'Seventy-seven on Friday and seventy six on Saturday.'

Mr Barnes stood silent for a moment, deep in thought.

'I think I can see what's happened,' he said after a while.

'Many of the stones in the circle are very similar to one another. I imagine that John made his drawing at one particular spot, and when he returned on Saturday he was looking at a different set of stones that bore a close resemblance to those he sketched.'

'But what about the fresh piece of turf?' asked Simon.

'I'm sure with all the visitors that go to look at the Stones, it's necessary from time to time to replace turf where it's been worn away. I think your imagination has tended to run away with you a little. Besides I hardly think anyone would want to steal one. What use would they be? Still, I'm very pleased that you made the effort to go back there in your own time. Now shall we get on? Today we're going to have a look at another megalithic circle at Avebury in Wiltshire. If you look in your atlases you'll find it ...'

Break-time found Sarah, John and Simon huddled against the wind on the far side of the playground.

'That was a sodding stupid thing to do!' exclaimed John angrily. 'Letting our secrets out in front of everyone!'

'Oh shut up!'

'I reckon Mr Barnes was right,' said Simon. 'You probably imagined it, John.'

'I did not!'

Sarah looked across the playground. The distant figure of Mr Taylor could be seen patrolling the yard. Heading towards them were Stuart Crawford and his cronies.

'I think John was right,' said Sarah. 'I don't care what Mr Barnes or anyone else says, I think we should get to the bottom of it!'

'Perhaps I was wrong.' John didn't sound too sure of himself anymore.

'No you're not!' said Sarah vehemently. 'We'll show them. There's something funny going on and I reckon we need to find out a lot more about the Rollright Stones!'

'How can you do that?' asked Simon. He often wondered where teachers obtained their limitless store of facts and information.

'Easy!' said Sarah, 'Mr Barnes is always telling us about using the library. He told us he got most of his information from Warwick. I reckon I'll go over and have a browse around. They stay open until eight o'clock at night.'

'It'll be dark long before then,' warned Simon, 'and you'd never get a bus back for ages.'

'I hadn't thought of that,' agreed Sarah. 'I know, I'll go on Saturday.'

'Good,' said John protectively. 'We'll come along as well, just to look after you!'

Sarah grinned.

'OK Big Brother! Saturday morning!'

'I'll meet you at ten o'clock outside the Post Office,' said Simon.

'You know, it might be just my imagination...' began Sarah.

'Oh not your "funny feelings" again,' groaned John.

'No, but I've just remembered, while we were waiting for you to count the stones on Saturday, this woman ...'

Stuart Crawford arrived at that moment waving two fingers rudely at John.

'How many fingers am I holding up, Professor?' he gibed.

The ensuing fight lasted until Mr Taylor rang the bell and they all trooped back into the building.

Six

Sarah, John and Simon climbed aboard the bus. It was Saturday morning and the start of their outing to Warwick Library. There was an air of adventure about the expedition. No longer were they finding out facts just for school, theirs was now the role of investigator, searcher of secrets and hidden mysteries. Each of them now felt that there was something not quite right about the Stone Circle. Their education had included much imaginative talk, and the world of books had furnished them with fertile minds for searching out the extraordinary. It appeared in their writing in school, and these influences had laid a good foundation for them to realise how close the unexplained could lie to the everyday things of life.

Bubbling with their eagerness to get to grips with their task, they journeyed into Warwick. The ride was occupied with much surmising as to how and why the stone had disappeared. Light relief was provided when Simon tripped over his new high-heeled boots, first time on in honour of the occasion, and fell onto the conductor as they climbed downstairs from the top deck of the bus.

The town of Warwick buzzed with cars and people. Simon, Sarah and John gathered on the pavement as the bus moved off.

'Right! Let's ask where the library is then,' said Simon, gazing dimly about him, in hopes of it leaping out and waving.

'Don't be daft.' said Sarah. 'We know where it is, we sometimes come with our Dad. He likes to get his history books from here. It's his hobby.'

They strolled quickly through the archway that led from Northgate Street, and entered the library. The front door opened into a corridor and to their right was the Junior Section. Doors to the left led to the Reference Library and the Reading Room. At the far end of the corridor was the Adult Lending Library.

'Are we allowed in there?' whispered Simon. Official places always made him feel nervous. It was like going to church. All those solemn grown-ups and no talking. Still he was with his friends, and they seemed to know what to do.

'I think so.' Sarah didn't sound quite sure.

'I know,' she continued hastily, anxious to reassert her superior knowledge of adult institutions. 'We'll ask in the Junior Section for a start.'

They opened the door and went inside. A woman appeared from behind a shelf of books.

'Can I help you?'

Sarah pushed past the boys.

'Yes, we're doing a project on Megalithic Circles and we were wondering if you had anything on the Rollright Stones?'

'Sarah and her Megalithy Whatsisnames,' thought Simon. 'That's the way to get service.'

'Oh I'm sure we'll have something.'

'Thanks.' Sarah turned to the others. 'Let's have a look at the books while we're waiting.'

They browsed around, idly picking up books and glancing through them.

'I'm afraid the only books we've got in the Junior Section are all about Stonehenge,' said the assistant, returning with two picture books.

Sarah's face registered disappointment.

'Oh!'

'Wasn't that the sort of thing you were looking for?'

'Well, not really. You see we've found out all the facts about Stonehenge and things, we wanted to know a bit more about the Rollrights. We live quite near and we've got interested in some of the stories we've heard about them.'

'I see.' The assistant thought for a few moments. 'I think we still may be able to help you, although the books we have are more for adults ...'

Sarah felt her blood-pressure rise. She knew a lot of grown ups who hadn't read half the books that she had. She fought back her annoyance and tried to smile.

'Yes, anything you've got would be useful.'

'If you go out into the corridor,' continued the assistant, 'turn first left and you'll find another part of the library. Go to the desk and ask the lady there if you can see the Warwick Collection. Tell her what you're looking for and she'll show you where the section is kept that you'll need.'

'Thanks!'

They hurried out of the room and into the doorway across the corridor. A girl sat stamping books at a desk.

'Can I help?'

'Well, the lady next door said you might have something in the Warwick Collection.'

'What sort of thing were you looking for?'

'Oh,' Sarah had forgotten to mention the subject of their search. 'We're doing a project on the Rollright Stones at school, and we live quite close and thought we'd like to find out a bit more about them.'

'Right, if you follow me we'll see what we can find. Are these two boys with you?'

'Yes,' replied Sarah diffidently. She half expected them to be refused entry.

'This way then.'

She led them up some wooden stairs to a set of rooms that smelled of old books and leather. Simon felt it was even more like a church.

'Come through this way.'

They stepped into a smaller room at the far end.

'Now here are all the books about folk-tales and superstitions in Warwickshire. Take care how you handle them,' she looked meaningfully at Simon and John. 'Over there are some files with private collections of papers that have been given to the library. Some of them go back more than a couple of hundred years, so take care!'

She headed back towards the stairs.

'I'll be downstairs if you should need any more help.'

Sarah scanned the titles on the shelf. They were all very old books, and none of them looked very exciting, unlike the colourful dust-covers that sparkled on the shelves of the Junior Library.

'Well, here goes.'

She picked one at random. John did the same. Simon, obviously bored by the scholarly turn that the proceedings had taken, whispered to John.

'I'm dying for a pee. I'll be back soon.'

He scuttled away, his new boots clumping against the uncarpeted stairs. Red-faced he stole past the amused gaze of the assistant librarian.

Upstairs the rooms were quiet. The hum of traffic was muted and Sarah and John dipped into the dusty and mouldering pages of the old books that retold the ancient legends of the county. Time passed.

Sarah suddenly sat up and poked John in the ribs.

'Hey!'

'Listen to this!' Sarah was keeping her place amongst the forest of old print. 'It says here that Long Compton has a history of witch-craft going back to the thirteenth century and even earlier.'

'What's that got to do with the Stones?'

'I don't know, but listen, it says that in the thirteenth century Saint Augustine...'

'Saint Who?'

'Saint Augustine. He visited Long Compton and was taking a service there, and there was a Knight who wouldn't give his share to the church as a thanksgiving for Harvest. He reckoned that as he and his men had done all the planting and reaping, he deserved all the profits.'

'So what happened?'

'This Knight was in the congregation when Saint Augustine was preaching his sermon, and when he mentioned that people who did not give their rightful tithe to God should be cast out of the church there was this terrible scream in the churchyard and a body rose from its grave and ran out of the church grounds.'

'Go on!'

'Saint Augustine ran out of the church after it and he was followed by the Knight who had refused to pay his tithe. Saint Augustine caught up with the corpse and demanded to know who he was. The corpse told him that he had been a vain farmer some hundred and fifty years before, and had not believed in giving his portion to the church. The priest had excommunicated him and he had languished in Hell for all those years, until that day.'

Sarah rolled the grand phrases around her lips.

'Saint Augustine then raised the dead priest who was buried nearby and asked him if this was correct. The priest agreed that it was true. Saint Augustine then asked the corpse what it had been like in hell, and at this it gave out such a terrible groan that Saint Augustine forgave it, and it returned to its grave, and its soul was saved.'

'What happened to the priest?'

'Well, it says that Saint Augustine gave him the choice of returning to earth to help save more sinners, or going back to heaven. The priest said he was happy in heaven so Saint Augustine returned him to his grave as well.'

'And what happened to the Knight who wouldn't pay his tithe?'

'Oh, he was so terrified that he paid up immediately and Saint Augustine forgave him too.'

John stared at Sarah.

'Just think, all that happening in the churchyard at Long Compton! I won't be going there on my own in a hurry. Do you reckon it's true?'

'I don't know, but it gives you a funny sort of feeling, doesn't it? I mean, things seem to have been happening there for a long time.'

'You don't think our missing stone had anything to do with that sort of thing do you? Ghosts and all that?' John had begun to look a little worried.

Sarah shrugged.

'I suppose not.'

'Come on, let's see if we can find anything else.'

Footsteps clattered up the stairs, heralding the return of the incontinent Simon. A grin was pasted across his face. From his pocket he pulled three packets of crisps.

'One for each of us!'

With great relish he pulled open one of the packets and began to cram the contents into his mouth.

'Don't do that!' hissed Sarah. 'You'll get us all thrown out!'

Simon looked crestfallen. Sarah suddenly felt rather sorry for him. It had been a kind thought after all.

'Thanks a lot, but we'd best eat them when we get outside,' she said.

'We've found some spooks!' said John with relish.

'Yeah?' Simon brightened up. 'Tell us about them then.'

'Later,' said Sarah firmly. 'We haven't finished yet.'

They pored through a dozen books or so whilst Simon busied himself as a self-appointed cleaner of dust from the files and bookshelves.

'God, it ain't half dusty!'

'I can't seem to find much about the stones at all,' sighed Sarah. 'It's all the stories that we know already, like the one about the man who tried to move the Kingstone down the hill and who gave up. Then there's the old rhyme about the stones being a King and his army that were turned to stone by a witch. That's about all.'

'You don't believe that story do you?' inquired John.

'No ....'

John looked across at Sarah. She seemed to be in a daydream.

'.... and yet .....'

'What do you mean "and yet"?'

'Well, I didn't think much about it until today, with Mr Barnes just telling us about it in school but I don't know now. Finding it all written out in these old books, like that story of Saint Augustine. Somebody other than schoolchildren must have believed it, or it wouldn't be in these books now.'

'Go on with you!' said John, half smiling.

'You see, John, all those stories must have started somewhere, and I've got a funny feeling that ...'

'Sarah!' interrupted John sharply. 'Mr Barnes said the Rollright Stones are a megalithic circle, probably a meeting place or something like that. Those stones were carried there by men, not magicked by ghosts and witches!'

'Oh, you're probably right!'

A few minutes elapsed. The sound of Simon's breath being expelled in far corners of the room, followed by violent bouts of coughing indicated that his human vacuum cleaner effect had disturbed a larger cloud of dust than anticipated.

'Hey Sarah!'

It was Sarah's turn to look up. John was peering at a page of print, not in a book, but a cutting from a yellowed newspaper fastened to a large file of dusty papers.

'See this.'

Sarah moved over to look.

'Arrested for the hideous and cold-blooded murder of Jane Shipton,' she read.

'Master John Woodward was accused of stabbing to death with a pitchfork one Jane Shipton of Clark's Lane, Long Compton on 15th September 1875. Woodward, a weak-minded man, had worked as a labourer at a nearby farm, and being deluded into the thought that the many troubles that had lately afflicted the village were due to the influence of witches, had murdered the old woman and named her and sixteen others in the village as equally to blame, and worthy of burning. He claimed that the water he had drunk was infected with witches and that his body had been cursed so that he was unable to work. He demanded that the body of Jane Shipton be weighed against the Church Bible to prove the truth of his statement. During his imprisonment pending trial Woodward requested a glass phial and stopper. These were provided and he then proceeded to fill the container with his urine. On inverting the phial a bubble formed in the liquid, and this, Woodward claimed, was firm evidence of his enchantment. He was found not guilty on the grounds of insanity, his simple-mindedness saving him from the gallows. He died some months later in Warwick Prison still protesting the justness of his action.'

'Whew!' Sarah sat back. 'There's certainly more in Long Compton than meets the eye.'

'Clark's Lane,' said John. 'That's just across the road from the Red Lion. We cycle past it on the way to the Rollright Stones.'

'That's right! God, and to think it only happened just over a hundred years ago! People still believed in witches in those days! What do you make of it John?'

'I don't rightly know,' he replied. 'But I think there is something weird about the place. I reckon we should leave things as they are. We haven't found anything more about the Stones anyway.'

'Oh, I found that bit about how the Stones are sometimes said to walk down the hill to drink at the stream at the bottom.'

'Oh that! You don't reckon that's what happened to the missing one do you? It got thirsty and toddled off for a drink? Perhaps it fancied something stronger and nipped into the pub!' John laughed at his joke.

'Maybe it did do something like that!' Sarah retorted.

'And the witches magicked it away! A likely story!' said John.

'No, not that exactly, but I've got this strange feeling that those old stories might have something to do with its disappearance.'

'What? Ghosts and witches and things that go bump in the night?'

'Something like that.'

'You and your ideas!'

Sarah turned away. She felt a strange prickling inside her eyelids as if tears were about to form.

'Come on let's go and eat those crisps that Simon bought.'

Simon appeared, dusty smears on his face. They clumped down the stairs.

'Bye, thanks for your help!'

The assistant smiled. 'Cheerio!'

Simon halted beside her.

'I cleaned up some of yer books for yer,' he grinned. 'Yer want to get a duster up there!'

They blinked their eyes as they emerged into the daylight. Sarah blew her nose. That strange tearful feeling had gone.

She was too imaginative that was her trouble. Her Dad would often warn her of nightmares when she was in this sort of mood. Still it had been a strange sensation that she'd never felt before. Wait a minute though, the feeling she had had at the Stones when that woman had told them off about picnicking. That had been a similar sort of thing. Her Dad had a saying for feelings like that, "Somebody walking over your grave." Sarah thought of Long Compton graveyard and the story of Saint Augustine. She shivered.

'What shall we do now?'

'John and me thought we'd nip over to Leamington and watch the football,' said Simon.

'Oh!'

Suddenly she didn't want to be left alone in this strange mood.

John sensed Sarah's unease.

'Do you want to come with us?'

Sarah shook her head.

'No, it's OK. I'll get back and make Dad's tea. Don't be late back, John.'

'Right.' John felt he needed to make up for leaving his sister in this manner. 'I tell you what, how about us going up to Long Compton tomorrow and having a good look around the village? We could have a look at Clark's Lane, and the churchyard!'

Sarah thought for a moment. 'Sounds a good idea. We might find something about the witches.'

'Witches?' Simon butted in.

'I'll tell you on the way to the match,' said John.

'So long, Sarah, don't forget your crisps.'

'See you tomorrow. Don't forget, John, don't be late home!'

They were gone, lost in the throng of shoppers. Sarah walked slowly towards the bus stop. 'Somewhere in all these stories I bet there's an answer' she told herself, and she shivered as the cold goose-pimple feeling swept swiftly over her once again.

Seven

They stood under the lych-gate of Long Compton Church. A tiny room perched over the gateway. Beneath its crumbling exterior Sarah, John and Simon discussed their findings.

'You can just imagine that story about Saint Augustine.' said Sarah, gazing rather fearfully at the gravestones that stood out of the grass at infrequent intervals. Most of the graves at the front of the church had long been overgrown and only occasionally did a headstone lurch upward out of the ground.

At the front of the church near the main road, a row of gigantic tree stumps stood guard, their heavy swirling trunks threatening the lone passer-by.

The churchyard was empty of visitors, but at the back of the church the sound of shovel and pick echoed. The children saw two men clad in dark overalls busily digging a grave. Sarah shuddered. The ritual starkness of the act made her think of the numberless times the task had been performed, right back to the times of Saint ....

'Let's go and ask them some questions!' John interrupted her thoughts. 'I bet they know some weird tales!'

He stepped across the grass.

'Excuse me, but we're doing a project in school about the witches of Long Compton and all those stories ....'

The two men stopped work. They seemed glad of the respite. Although it was a frosty morning the digging had produced a sweat on the reddened face of the older man. When he answered his voice was hard.

'It's not many as knows them old fairy-tales nowadays,' he muttered. 'If you'd be wanting a history of the village you'd best see the vicar, he's written a book about it, but I doubt you'll find much attention paid to daft tales of witches and the like.'

He turned to his colleague who spat on his hands and picked up his shovel, indicating that the interview as at an end.

'Friendly soul ... er ... oops!' whispered John, as he realised the aptness of his remark.

As they passed the church, Simon was attracted to a strange figure lying across one side of the porch. It was of human form, carved in the local stone, but the details of the face had been hideously distorted by years of weathering. It seemed an alien presence in a church doorway, a reminder of the legends of a time long since gone from the world.

'I don't think I like the look of that.' Simon seemed subdued. 'Do you reckon it's old Saint Whatsisname, him that got the dead ones out of their graves?'

'No,' John answered, 'I expect it's been left over from some old memorial. What do you think Sarah?' He turned towards his sister. Sarah stood forcing the knuckles of her hand into her mouth and gazing at the figure with a look of sheer terror in her eyes.

'Hey, what's the matter?'

She shook her head violently, and the look of fear faded.

'Nothing! Oh, come on, let's get out of here, that thing gives me the creeps!'

John looked at Simon. Together they hurried down the path to the roadway.

'Are you OK now?' asked John.

'Yes, I just felt, oh I don't know, sort of spooky. That figure. I felt as if I should know all about her, and what she was doing there, but that I'd forgotten it all and couldn't bring it back to mind. It frightened me.'

'Oh come on, forget it,' said John. 'You don't half get yourself worked up. I tell you what, let's go and find Clark's Lane, the site of a juicy murder will do wonders at cheering you up! It's just up the road past the Red Lion.'

They followed the winding road along heavy walls of Cotswold stone until the inn came into view. Just ahead a new petrol station gleamed in its livery of bright yellow and red.

'It's on the left,' said John, pointing.

Across the main road a small lane led off at right angles, skirted by small cottages and fenced orchards.

'Shall we walk down?'

Sarah and Simon nodded, and, crossing the road they edged down the lane, avoiding the large areas of mud that had been thrown up into miniature walls by the passage of tractors and other vehicles. A row of small cottages with leaded windows and the grey texture of local stone came into sight.

'Is it worth going any further?' Sarah seemed oddly disturbed by the place.

'Let's just go to where the road bends to the right. I expect it ends up in someone's back garden,' replied John.

The sharp fragrance of wood-smoke hit their nostrils, and at the bottom of the lane they saw a man dressed in old gardening clothes feeding a fire of decayed twigs and leaves. In his hand he grasped a pitchfork.

'Oh my God!'

Sarah bit her lip. For a moment she had thought they had been transported in time and were looking at Master Woodward on his way to carry out his terrible deed.

'Hey, it really isn't worth going any further is it?' pleaded Simon, tugging at John's arm. He too had noticed the figure and the coincidence had also registered with him.

'Oh come on!' John pushed ahead. 'He can't harm us. He's just an old man burning leaves.'

The images melted from their eyes and he came into focus just as John had described him. They hopped over puddles until they came to his bonfire.

'Excuse me.'

'Yes?'

'Er, well, we were wondering if you know anything about the witches that used to live around here?'

'Oh,' thought Sarah, 'that was rather blunt and to the point.'

The old man turned and ruffled the pitchfork thoughtfully through the burning leaves. He lifted some of the debris with it and turned it over. A cloud of acrid smoke enveloped the children.

'Afraid I can't help you.'

'Another one who doesn't want to talk about it,' thought John.

'You see I've not lived here that long,' the old man continued. 'I've just retired from North Wales as a matter of fact. Witches did you say? I'll have to behave myself if there's some of them around, won't I?' He laughed heartily at his joke.

'Thanks anyway,' said John when the explosion had died down.

'You're welcome. But look, if you want to ask someone who might know, why don't you ask at the house on the corner? See that gentleman in the garden, he hails from these parts, he might be able to help you.'

They looked back up the lane. Standing in the garden of the large corner house they saw a man, aged about thirty, with bright red hair.

'No harm in trying,' said John. 'Come on, if we don't find out anything this time I reckon we ought to head for home.'

'Right,' said Sarah and Simon together and they walked quickly to the end of the lane.

Sensing that they wished to talk with him, the man in the garden moved towards the fence.

'Hello, what do you youngsters want?' he spoke in the slow drawl of the county.

'Oh hello,' said Sarah, a little breathlessly. 'We were just talking to your neighbour.'

'Ah, that'd be Mr Llewellyn, he's new to these parts, from North Wales I believe.'

'Yes, that's right,' said John. 'Carry on Sarah.'

'We were just asking him if he knew anything about the witches that were supposed to have lived in Long Compton. You see we've been doing some work on the Rollright Stones in school and we got rather interested in the village. We thought someone might know something, living in Clark's Lane ...'

'Why Clark's Lane?' asked the man sharply.

'Oh because that's where the murder happened,' blurted out John.

He received a venomous glance from Sarah which made him kick himself for having let out their secret information.

'I see. Well my name's Dave Coulbeck. I used to live out towards Chipping Camden, but my wife and I have been here close on three years now. Look, why don't you come in and have a warm drink. I was just about to make a cup of tea. Come on in and we can have a good old chat.'

Sarah and John exchanged glances.

'Thanks very much.'

They followed him along the opposite side of the fence until they reached the garden gate. The inside of the house was warm and inviting, with thick carpets, and comfortable furniture.

'Make yourselves at home,' said Dave Coulbeck. 'I'll go and get some tea. Sit down by the fire. I expect you'll be glad of a warm.'

They sat on the floor in front of a huge log fire that burned cheerily in the old fireplace. Gradually they began to relax and examine their surroundings. Dave returned with a tray of biscuits and mugs of steaming tea.

'Here you are.' He handed them round.

'Now what have you been finding out about the witches then?'

Sarah and John had already come to the conclusion that Dave was to be trusted, and they quickly filled in the details of Master Woodward's deadly attack on the old lady. However, they did not go into the story of the missing stone. For some reason they felt that it was best left unmentioned as yet. When they finished their stories Dave sat back in a large arm-chair in front of the fire and stretched his long legs.

'Well I think you've earned your tea, for I haven't heard the details of those stories told so well since I have lived here.'

'So you knew them already?'

'Aye, well in a way. You see I've been rather interested in those stories myself, but it's taken me longer than you to get that far. It's nice to know that there's a grain of truth in some of these tales.'

'How did you find out about them then?' asked John. 'I suppose people would tell you easily enough, seeing as you're a grown-up.'

'Now that's a funny thing,' replied Dave. 'You see I found it the Devil's own job, if you'll pardon the expression, just to get any of the locals to talk at all. All they wanted to tell me were the tourist tales like that of Dick Whittington.'

Simon wanted to ask about that but the other two shushed him to silence. Dave continued.

'Anyroad, I was in the bar at the Red Lion a few times when this old man, now what's his name? Nearly eighty he is, Bill Jeffs, that's it. His family have lived in the village for over two hundred years he reckons. Well, it was late one night and the lads were just finishing their game of dominoes. Old Bill Jeffs, he likes his dominoes, and he plays mostly with the young lads. He's in there all hours, lunch time, supper time, right up until they close. This particular night he mustn't have been in the mood for playing anymore. The young 'uns had been ragging him about never buying his round, you know the sort of thing. We got to talking about the village and he told me some of the stories concerning witches, all very hushed and whispered like his conversation was, almost as if he were afraid of being overheard. Anyhow, he told me those tales you mentioned. How there were said to be enough witches in Long Compton to pull a wagon load of hay up the Hill, and the story you just told me about Saint Augustine and the dead man, although he didn't tell it in such detail as you've done.'

'Ah, we got that from an old book in Warwick Library,' said Sarah. 'It must be right.'

'Old Bill Jeffs was well away by this time,' continued Dave. 'He was whispering even more quietly and he told me that there was a story concerning his great, great, great grandfather, or even further back, he couldn't remember himself, and how he'd gone to help a farmer friend of his move the Kingstone from up the Rollrights.'

At the mention of the Rollrights the children leaned forward and listened more intently.

'It seems as how they got a team of horses to pull it down the hill, but with one thing and another they couldn't manage it so this farmer decides to cut his losses and take it back. They'd just harnessed the first horse again when it broke away and bolted up the hill, dragging the stone at a mighty pace back up to the circle. His great, great, great grandfather or whatever reckoned it weighed close to three ton and that no horse could pull that sort of weight. Seemed a bit daft to me, told as it was after a couple of pints. Anyway he went on to tell me that a woman from the village whom everyone believed to be a witch got rather angry when his ancestor started telling people about the magical powers of the Kingstone. She put a curse on him, and the village schoolmaster tried to raise it. Bill Jeffs didn't tell me whether he was successful or not, but he gave me the idea that ever since that day the witch had held some power over his family. As I said, it was an Old Wives Tale told over a couple of pints, but after he told me Old Bill got real feared of having let it slip and begged me not to mention it to anyone else. I gave it no heed, but you mentioned just now a man who tried to bridge yonder culvert and I'm thinking it might well have been him.'

Sarah, John and Simon sat transfixed.

'What else did he tell you?' asked Sarah in a faraway voice.

'I reckon that was about it. After he told me the tale he seemed to shut up completely, and soon after he went home. He doesn't live far from Clark's Lane as a matter of fact!'

'Have you ever asked him about any of the other stories?' inquired Sarah.

'No I haven't really had the chance. I don't get much opportunity for nipping out to the pub these days, what with the baby having arrived, and on the odd times I've gone into the bar he's usually been playing dominoes. I sent him over a drink the next time I was in, and he waved thank you, but that was all.'

'Hey! Do you reckon he'd be in the Red Lion now?' asked Simon.

Dave looked at his watch.

'Well they'll be closing for the afternoon in ten minutes. He'll probably be in there playing dominoes until then.'

John leapt to his feet, followed by Simon and Sarah.

'You're not going to find him are you?' said Sarah, carefully replacing her empty mug on the tray in front of the fire.

'Oh come on, let's.' said John. 'He might tell us something, you never know!'

Now whatever you do,' warned Dave, 'don't tell him that you know about the business with his great-great-great-grandfather and the witch.'

'But we know about the Kingstone being dragged back up the hill already, from our notes in school, all except about the witch's curse.'

'I wonder what sort of hold she had over him,' pondered Sarah.

'Thanks for the tea and the chat anyway,' said John politely.

'Don't forget what I said,' repeated Dave. 'Don't tell him you know about what he told me. He might be a bit touchy.'

'OK. Thanks again!'

As he let them out of the door Dave paused.

'You want to know what I think about it?' he asked.

The three children stopped and listened.

'I reckon there's something queer still going on in this village.'

'How do you mean, queer?' asked Simon.

'I'm not too sure, but by the way I hear people talk and the way Bill Jeffs acts I wouldn't be a bit surprised if it had to do with the Old Ways.'

'The Old Ways?' echoed Sarah.

'Aye.'

Dave looked into her eyes and for a moment the strange prickling of tears troubled her again.

'The Old Ways. Some call it Witchcraft.'

She looked at him, wide eyed.

He realised that he'd probably gone too far in frightening them. After all, they were only children.

'No, I'm most likely mistaken,' he shrugged. 'It's no more than me being a newcomer I expect. Now off you go and see if Old Bill can tell you some tales.'

They thanked him again and hurried to the main road and across into the car park of the Red Lion. The door to the bar was visible and they stood waiting to see if anyone would emerge. Inside a bell tinkled and a woman's voice called out.

'Last orders please!'

'What are you going to say to him if he comes out?' asked Simon a little apprehensively.

'What we always say,' said Sarah in a rather blasé fashion.

'We'll tell him about our project. We won't ask him outright about the witches in case we frighten him off.'

At that moment the bar door opened and a group of young men with long hair and wearing denim jackets appeared, laughing and joking, they walked off down the road.

'That's it then,' said Simon. 'It doesn't look like Old Bill was in there.'

The door opened again and an old man emerged wearing an ancient cap, the peak pulled down over his face.

'That must be him!' hissed John. 'Come on, after him!'

The old man had reached the pavement and had set off briskly down the road. The three children hurried after him, and putting on an extra spurt John overtook and turned to face him.

'Excuse me, we're from Roddwych School,' announced John with the ease of long practice. 'We're doing some work on the Rollright Stones and we thought that perhaps some of the older people in the village might know some interesting stories about them.'

The old man stopped. His chin was covered in partly shaved stubble, and his breath smelled of stale beer.

'I don't know anything about any stones,' he muttered.

'Oh, well, I'm sorry to have bothered you,' said John hurriedly, beginning to lose his nerve.

'Thanks anyway, Mr Jeffs!' said Simon brightly. Poor old sod, he was almost senile, he obviously didn't know anything!

A thin but wiry hand grasped Simon by the arm.

'How did yer know my name, sonny?' The old man spat the words.

Sarah looked at John in horror. Simon was bound to tell him about Dave Coulbeck and the stories they'd heard.

'Me Gran knows yer!' said Simon with commendable quickness of thought. 'She used to live 'ere a few years back.'

Sarah knew this to be a blatant untruth, but the tone of Simon's voice and the obvious familiarity of the answer seemed to satisfy the old man.

'Them old stones,' he mused. 'Used to tell us to keep well away when I was in school. You'd best be advised to do the same!'

'Don't you know any stories at all about them?' asked John, beginning to regain some of his confidence.

'Maybe I do, maybe I don't,' replied the old man querulously. 'Why do yer want to know?'

'For school, for some work for school,' repeated Sarah loudly.

'Oh aye, for school. Well it'll do no harm I suppose.'

The children drew nearer to him and listened. He told them the tale he had told Dave Coulbeck, the story of his long forgotten great-great-great grandfather, and the moving of the Kingstone. This time however, he did not mention the witch or her strange curse. Neither did he say anything about the stone being returned by only one horse.

'So they never actually used the stone?' prompted Sarah gently.

'No, it weren't the right size.'

'Did they take it back then?' John queried, a little more pointedly.

'They must've done, mustn't they? It's still there ain't it?' Bill Jeffs seemed keen to end his reminiscing.

'Thanks for sparing us so much time, Mr Jeffs,' said Sarah finally. His tale had been interesting but the ending had changed, and they had found out no more than they knew already. What was so important about a stone being returned by one horse and the ridiculous curse of an old woman long ago? Even if it was true in the first place, which was highly unlikely!

'Yer don't want to go filling yer heads with all that rubbish about them stones anyway!' rasped the old man.

'What rubbish?' asked John, taken aback by this fresh outburst.

'Them stories of the King and his Knights.'

Bill Jeffs had suddenly begun to talk rapidly. The children bent forward to listen. It seemed as if once again he had felt he had told too much and was trying to talk his way out of it. Sarah wondered if his excuses might lead him inadvertently to reveal further tales. They listened attentively. Sarah led him along, questioning him gently.

'You mean those stories about the circle being a King and his army turned to stone?'

The old man seemed lost in a reverie. He muttered, half to himself.

'Don't want to take no notice of them old tales. No one can give them life, and I reckon her that says so is out of her right mind, fortune or no fortune, and that's an end. She's no hold on me and that's a fact.'

'Pardon?' said Sarah and John simultaneously. They had only caught a few of his words and they didn't make sense. Give them life? And had he mentioned a fortune?

He looked at the children and his eyes re-focused.

'That's all I can remember. When you've lived as long as me you'll find it hard to recall yer schoolin'. Now I've got to get off. Ma Shipton don't like me to be late.'

He strode past them, remarkably agile for a man of his years. The three children stood looking at one another.

'What do you make of that?' asked John when Bill Jeffs was safely out of sight. 'A different ending to his story, and didn't he mention something about a fortune?'

'That's right,' said Simon. 'Something about giving them life and her that says so being mad, fortune or no fortune.'

'What's a fortune got to do with it?' said John, baffled. 'I don't get that at all. The stories don't mention fortunes.'

'Perhaps it's just his way of talking,' explained Simon, 'you know, like when we say "Bet yer any money".'

'Could be,' replied John. 'What do you reckon Sarah?'

The two boys glanced at her. To their surprise she was crying.

'What's the matter?' asked John. 'What are you crying for?'

'Yer not upset are yer?' said Simon, concerned. He fished out his handkerchief. Tears rolled down Sarah's face. She was shivering and her skin was raised into goose-pimples.

'Thanks Simon. I don't know what's the matter. It was that feeling again, and I just started to cry.'

'But why?' asked John. 'He didn't do anything to upset you, did he?'

'Not exactly.' Sarah blew her nose and handed the handkerchief back to Simon. 'It was just something he said. I'm all right now.'

'You mean you got upset by his stories? The bit about them being given life and her that believed it being round the bend?'

'No!'

Sarah almost shouted in their faces.

'Not when he was talking about the stories, just before he walked away.'

'Eh?' Simon and John looked blankly at Sarah.

'He said "Ma Shipton doesn't like me to be late".'

'What's wrong with that?' asked John.

'Don't you remember?' Sarah's eyes refilled with tears and they flooded down over her cheeks.

'Remember what?' chorused the boys.

'In Warwick Library. The story of the murdered witch. Remember her name? It was Jane Shipton!'

Eight

The hand that closed the curtain lit the candles.

The Watchers stood.

In the soft glow of candle-light the Stone waited.

Muttered talk was silenced.

She stood before them. Her hands reached out to touch the Stone. Again the candles flared and died.

'The time is right,' the voice echoed through the room. The Stone stood proudly, its moss and lichen cleaned. It rested on a cloth of darkest blue. A royal colour.

She spoke the Words.

This time there was power in her voice. The Watchers stood back aghast, for with this power came noises, purged from Hell. A cry of tortured rage, almost beyond endurance. All eyes were fixed on the Stone.

The Words continued. The Power grew. Now, as if at the height of a storm, the air crackled and leapt. The door latches rattled and the tables and chairs vibrated. A smell of charred earth grew stronger.

The Watchers stood.

A cacophony of sound. A flame leapt from the Stone and within its violent heart a light of great intensity was formed. Within its core the outline of the Stone re-emerged. Gone was the craggy shape, the cleaned crevices of limestone. In its place was revealed the terrible vision of a face, not of our time, its eyes dark and its pupils drowned. It glared briefly, as if grimacing at its rebirth, and with awful slowness its glowing eyelids closed and opened. And suddenly it was gone. The flame had died. The whitened hands reached out.

'Now are there any doubts?' her voice was still strong.

The Watchers were silent.

'Come, there is much to arrange.'

The Watchers followed her from the room.

The blue velvet lay charred upon the table.

The Stone cooled.

They sat around a table. The Watchers white and trembling. One muttered to himself as if the experience had driven him from his senses. She did not wait for them to regain their composure. She had waited too long for this day. She must speak now while the Power was active. She must guide and command, and they must obey.

'The Power was with me! The Lore has not changed.' Her voice was firm and clear.

'I have told the Lore these many years, and guided my followers, as did my mother before me, and her mother before that. The Words of Power have been handed down through many generations.'

The Watchers nodded in agreement.

'For a thousand years or more we in this village have worshipped the darker powers of the Earth, and by our obedience we have been repaid with prosperity and healthy families. Each generation has provided its Watchers, to learn and be guided by the Shipton of that time. By our unfailing worship we have been given control of the earth's most basic powers. Yet few in the past have given credit where it has been due! When plague ravaged our homes the villagers grovelled to their new found Christian God! Few recognised the real source of their protection! So it has been these many years. Few in the village would now give credence to our beliefs, yet you Watchers, chosen by your predecessors have kept the Power strong. All praise to you! Today for the first time in *your* lives you have seen the Power manifest itself. You have seen the Stone transformed from dead and lifeless matter. Do any now doubt the Legend of the Rollright Stones?'

The Watchers shook their heads.

'Now mark my words. Any that shall speak unguarded beyond our coven from this day will do so at their peril!'

The old man shuffled nervously in his seat.

She reached across the table and lifted from it a heavy leather-bound book, the pages yellowed and crumbling with age. She opened it carefully and revealed a page of closely written script.

'For many centuries the Lore that has aided this village has been handed down within my family alone, and we have done all we can to preserve the rightful majesty of those darker powers. But now I am old and sick and I bear no family to pass on my gifts. Thus have I decided to bestow to you, the last Watchers of the village, some store of knowledge, that you may together benefit before my passing. For with me end the Old Ways of Long Compton.'

The Watchers sat silent.

'Tonight the Words of Power imparted life to one of the Stones, for it was the Words of Power that first transformed them from living flesh, and my true ancestor who did the deed. Now listen well. Marked within my book lies tell of that which for countless years was left unwritten, but handed down by word of mouth to each of Shipton's brood. When the King was translated to his stony rest, some faithless jackal of the Royal Court, at first escaping from the Words of Power, returned upon the scene. He was met by the Watchers of the village, and so it seems his senses were deranged, yet before the Power parted him from life he raved of stones, of which you would expect, but also of a treasure, newly hid, an Act of Appeasement to their savage gods.'

She paused to let her words sink in.

'And now, as such powers that I hold shall die with me, and my kind shall no longer be present to protect the village, then crude wealth must take the place of Magic.

We shall return the King to life, and he shall tell us of the place of Appeasement, and the riches shall be ours to keep our village strong!'

'Great riches,' she repeated.

'But where?' questioned the old man.

'The exact place was not known to humble soldiers but to the King alone. Our words must be with him. Now that you have witnessed the Power you must bring him to me, for only here will my persuasion prove strong enough.'

She smiled tightly.

'I shall call you again, when the King is brought to me.'

The Watchers rose from the table.

A figure detached itself from the rest and approached her.

'I warn of meddlers Mother.'

She looked directly into the eyes of the speaker.

'Who?'

'Some children have been seen, asking questions of ...' his voice trailed away.

'Continue!'

'... witches, and stories of the Stones.'

'Children?'

'Yes Mother. Three. Two boys and a girl.'

'I hardly think our work concerns the minds of infants!'

She waved her hand in dismissal.

The Watchers left.

'Children!'

She entered the room, the stone was now cold to her touch.

'Children!'

What effect could they have on her plans? Yet she was unsure of herself. The past few weeks had brought a feeling of unease, and the manifestation of her Power tonight had in some ways been incomplete. The transformation had been all too brief. Yet it had been but a common soldier! When she had the King! Ah, yes! When she had the King it would be different.

Nine

Sarah and John said goodbye to Simon at the Post Office and returned home. John put away their bicycles while Sarah busied herself preparing tea. Her mind whirled with the strange collection of fact and fiction which they had discovered, and she felt them merge until she could no longer remember clearly the source from which they came.

Bill Jeffs and his story of the returned stone, and the extra part about the witch's curse. The history of witchcraft in the village, and most disturbing of all the presence of a Ma Shipton still living in the neighbourhood. Surely that must be pure coincidence? Then of course there was the start of their quest – the missing Rollright Stone.

Sarah sighed. It was like some gigantic jig-saw puzzle. She felt that somewhere much of this information was connected. Had she missed anything? Of course, that strange figure in the porch, and the feeling she had of knowing about it. She shuddered and thought of the unhelpful gravediggers. There were certainly some strange happenings about the place, and people weren't very forthcoming either! Except Dave Coulbeck that was! What had he said as they left his house? 'I reckon there's something queer still going on in this village ... the Old Ways ... Witchcraft!' The strange prickling at the back of her eyelids returned momentarily. She blinked away the tears that were trying to form themselves. How stupid. She was really getting over-emotional! Yet she'd never had that feeling until the last few days. Since they'd been probing about the Stones to be exact. Still, she was at the awkward age, at least that was what Aunty Rose told her. Having no mother it fell to Aunty Rose to keep Sarah informed of the approaching horrors of adolescence, a role which she fulfilled with missionary zeal. Tantrums, hot flushes, the pains of her first period had all been dealt with at one time or another by well-meaning Aunty Rose. Although Sarah tended to dismiss most of her advice as old wives' tales, she had to admit that her moods and feelings were in a constant whirl, and these tearful outbursts could well be attributed to the changes she was going through.

They finished their tea and Sarah sat with her back against her father's chair, toasting her toes at the fire. John was upstairs putting the finishing touches to a model aeroplane that he had been working on for the past few weeks. Her father sat engrossed in a book. The room was warm and cosy, and Sarah felt relaxed and secure. She wondered idly what her father would make of all the tales. Her eyes glanced casually over the title of the book her father was reading. History again. It was a wonder he didn't get tired of it. Still, he knew lots of interesting facts about all sorts of things to do with the past. Perhaps if she mentioned their finds? But no, somehow she felt she didn't want to involve him in their secret.

'What are you reading, Dad?'

'Eh?' he grunted, and peered over the top of his book. 'What was that?'

'What are you reading?'

'Oh this?' he placed the book carefully on the coffee table beside his chair. It was an expensively bound volume with carefully drawn illustrations and coloured plates. 'It's all about the customs of the old Kings and their followers,' he said.

'Oh,' said Sarah. It sounded a little too dry for her taste. She picked up her own book and began to read.

'They were right daft 'uns, some of those old Kings,' said her father, picking up the heavy volume again.

Sarah glanced up. 'What was that, Dad?'

'Some of these old Kings had some weird ideas of winning battles.'

'How do you mean?'

'Well in those days, these Kings, although they weren't really Kings like we have nowadays of course, because Britain wasn't ruled by just one, the country was split up and shared between them. These Kings were always fighting amongst themselves for absolute power. They used to worship heathen gods. They believed in the spirits of earth, fire, water and so on. Before a battle they would arrange to throw all their valuable tackle, gold plate, jewels and the like, into a lake or a stretch of water to please the spirits. It was supposed to put them in good favour with their gods and help them win. The place they used was always kept a deadly secret. An Act of Appeasement is what this book says they called it. Daft sort of thing to do wasn't it? Yet they reckon that it was common practice until less than a thousand years ago.'

Sarah nodded absently.

'Like as not, next time some problem comes up in the shop,' her father continued, 'I'd best get out the silver knives and forks and chuck 'em down the nearest drain. Might bring me good luck!'

He stood up and stretched.

'Time for bed. School for you and John in the morning!'

Sarah closed her book and went and made three cups of coffee. When they were ready she took a cup in to her father and carried the other two upstairs. She took one into John's room and said goodnight, but John was too absorbed in his model making. She took her cup into her bedroom and closed the door.

The week passed quickly. Her father was kept busy in the shop most evenings and Sarah was also busy catching up on her homework which had been neglected the previous weekend. John and Simon had been similarly occupied and they only had chance to talk briefly about their findings. They decided that nothing more could be accomplished until the following weekend when they would visit Long Compton again.

The decision to visit the village again had been made by Sarah. She now felt some irresistible urge to return, and she went to some pains to convince the boys of the necessity of another visit. Although they were still interested she felt that their enthusiasm was waning, particularly as they had not really got much further with their quest.

The following Saturday morning found them again cycling through Long Compton.

'Where do we start?' asked John. 'I don't really see where we go from here.'

Sarah frowned. She too had her doubts. At the back of her mind a stray thought had been nagging all through the week, a misplaced piece of information. She had a feeling that she had overlooked some vital clue. She compared it to the experience she sometimes had when she went to do some shopping for her father. She would be certain that she had remembered all the items, yet when she returned home the most obvious thing had been forgotten.

'Let's just go up to the Circle and have a think,' she replied, for want of a better suggestion.

They cycled along the main road and approached Clark's Lane. In the garden of the corner house they saw a familiar figure. He waved to them as they sailed past. They braked and wobbled to a halt.

'Hello there!' called Dave Coulbeck.

'Hello!' they shouted back.

'Still hunting for old tales are you?' he asked.

They climbed off their bikes and leaned them against his garden fence.

'Did you manage to find Old Bill last week?'

'Oh yes,' said John. 'He told us the same story he told you.'

'Except he left out the ending,' reminded Sarah.

'Oh?'

'Yes, he didn't make any mention of how the stone got back to the circle. Or the witch's curse, and afterwards he seemed sorry he'd said so much.'

'Aye, he's a queer one, there's no doubt about that,' said Dave, shaking his head. 'Did he tell you anything else?'

'No, not really,' said Sarah, 'only to keep away from them. Oh, and something about giving them life, but it was all rather mixed up.'

'Did he indeed? Is that all he said?'

'Yes!' answered Sarah and John together.

'You know it was a funny thing you asking about those old stories last week,' continued Dave.

'Pardon?'

'Well, last Saturday night, about ten o'clock, the baby had settled down and we were sitting by the fire, when I suddenly had this fancy for a pint of beer, so I says to the wife, "I've got a rare thirst, would you mind if I popped down the local for a quick one?" Anyroad, I put on my coat and strolled across to the Red Lion. I gets my pint and I'm standing at the bar when I notice Bill Jeffs sitting in the corner. He seemed quieter than usual, and just then one of the young lads who he plays dominoes with passes by and says "G'night Bill". Old Bill just sort of looked at him a bit glassy-eyed. Then he turned to me and by his breath I can tell he's been seeing the bottom of a few glasses that evening and no mistake.

"Do yer want a drink then?" he asks, his voice all slurred.

"No" I replies, "I've only got the time for this one."

"I can afford it" he says and clutches hold of my sleeve.

"Aye, of course," I says, trying to calm him. "No offence."

"I might not look up to much," he goes on, "but I'll show 'em, I'll show 'em who'll have the bloody money!"

"Expecting a win on the Pools, eh?" I says, joking a bit, and he grabs my hand tighter.'

Simon remembered that wiry grasp.

"'I don't need no bloody Pools," he says. "There's more coming to me than bloody Pools money, you mark it!'"

Well by this time I'm ready for off, but he's still rambling on like the Devil.

"You was the one who was askin' about the old stories weren't yer?" he says all of a sudden. I nodded my head and he carried on, though he was muttering so low I had a job to pick out his every word.

"You know the tales of them stones don't yer?" he asks.

"Aye," I tells him.

"And yer know about me great great great grandfather who tried to move 'em?"

I nodded at him again.

"There's a lot more than that, you believe me." He was cackling now, just like an old hen. "They used to tell when I was a lad of that man who saw 'em turn, but I never believed 'em in those days."

This was a bit beyond me, but he carried on. "Me Gran would often tell us about him. He saw 'em turn. They found him and he were mad and talked of great fortune. And now she says it too, just like me Gran. He died though and no one knew. But she'll find out."

His voice trailed away then and I thought it was time to be off. As I rose to go he grabbed my sleeve again.

"She has no hold on me," he croaked, "not like some, I'm still me own man." He glanced around the bar, almost fearful, and I left him all hunched up in his corner. Pathetic he looked. What do you make of that?'

'Him that saw them turn,' said Sarah. 'Turn what?'

'The Stones!' exclaimed John. 'Him that saw them turned to stone!' His grammar lapsed in his excitement. 'It must have been someone who saw the King and his army turn to stone!'

'I never thought of that,' said Dave slowly. 'You could be right.'

'So he died,' said Sarah thoughtfully. 'He went mad and died.'

'I'm not surprised,' said Simon. 'Reckon if I'd seen that sort of thing happen I'd have gone doolally!'

Dave laughed.

'It was just another of his stories I expect. Still I'd like to know how he was so certain he was coming into money. I could do with a bit of that sort of fortune-telling myself.'

The nagging feeling inside Sarah's brain reasserted itself.

'Come on,' said Simon. 'I thought we were going up to the Circle?'

'Right,' said John. They climbed onto their bicycles.

Sarah seemed a million miles away. She pulled her bicycle from the fence.

'Cheerio then,' said Dave. 'See you again soon!'

'Does anybody called Shipton live hereabouts?' asked Sarah suddenly.

'Shipton, Shipton?' Dave furrowed his brown. 'Of course! Ma Shipton, she lives just down the bottom of the Lane, in the end cottage. Why? Do you know her?'

'No,' replied Sarah. 'No, but thanks anyway.'

'Didn't think you could have,' said Dave. 'She's a strange one, she keeps herself to herself as far as we're concerned. Mind, some of the locals drop in to see her quite often, they certainly think a lot of her. I often see them going down the Lane on their way to call on her.'

Simon and John tinkled their bells impatiently.

'Bye then,' called Dave.

Sarah nodded to him. Her mind was racing, as the chains of circumstance finally forged together and the answer stared her in the face.

Ten

Sarah's thoughts kept her busy as they struggled up Long Compton Hill. The way was familiar now and Simon kept up a barrage of chatter which saved her from speaking until their breath was required for the final pull up to the turning to the Rollright Stones.

They free-wheeled the remaining few hundred yards to the lay-by and dumping their bicycles on the ground, they collapsed in a breathless heap on the grass verge.

Sarah's eyes were sparkling with tears but this time she paid no heed to the now familiar pricking beneath her eyelids.

'I think I've worked it out!' she exploded.

John and Simon turned to stare at her.

'The other night, last Saturday as a matter of fact, I was sitting by the fire with Dad while you were upstairs finishing off your model. He was reading this old history book about the ancient Kings and their customs. He started to tell me about this daft idea they had called an Act of ...' She grasped for the right word 'an Act of Appeasement. You see they used to worship the powers of earth, air, fire and water, and just before a battle the King would throw all their valuables, like gold and treasure and so on, into a lake or stretch of water as a gift to their gods, so that they would be victorious.'

John and Simon listened, not quite sure what to make of the information.

'Can you see what that's got to do with the missing stone, Simon?' asked John, turning to where Simon lay stretched out on the damp grass.

Simon shook his head, but continued to look at Sarah, wanting her to continue.

'Let me finish! Just tell me this. What sort of people were the stones supposed to have been?'

'That's easy,' answered Simon happy that the conversation had at last found its way back to solid fact. 'They were a King and his soldiers.'

'Exactly!'

'So?'

'Wait a minute,' John butted in.

Sarah waited eagerly. She desperately wanted John to work it out for himself. If he came to the same conclusion she would feel even more convinced of the truth of her theory.

John was fumbling for words.

'The story of the King and his army. The King wanted to be King of all England, so he must have been on his way to a battle!'

'Right!'

'And the King and his men would have believed in this Act of Appeasement?'

Sarah nodded frantically.

John's words tumbled out.

'So they would have disposed of their treasure before they were turned to stone! But it would have to have been in water!'

'That's it!' exclaimed Sarah.

'But what's that got to do with nowadays?' asked Simon, puzzled.

'Don't you see?' cried Sarah. 'The history of witchcraft in the village. The witch turned them to stone. She probably wanted to get her hands on the treasure for herself.'

'Perhaps she did,' said John. 'You'll never know.'

'Wait a minute though,' whispered Sarah. 'If you remember, the witch was turned into an elder tree at the same time. Something must have gone wrong with her magic. She would never have had a chance to find out!'

Simon and John slowly digested the fact.

'So the hiding place of the treasure remained a secret.'

Sarah nodded.

'Well that's it then,' said Simon.

'It's a fantastic theory of yours, Sarah,' conceded John, 'but it brings the story to rather a dead end, doesn't it?'

'I haven't finished yet,' hissed Sarah impatiently. 'Remember Bill Jeff's words? "Him that saw them turn"?'

'What's that got to do with it?' said John.

'Him that saw 'em turn.' repeated Sarah. 'He would have known about the treasure. It wasn't a woman that Bill Jeffs mentioned, the witch had already turned into an elder tree. He told Dave about a *man* who saw them turn.'

'Hey I think you're onto something,' gasped John. 'Him who saw them turn.' What were Bill Jeff's words again? 'They found him and he were mad, and he talked of great fortune.'

'That's right,' said Sarah excitedly. 'He must have meant the treasure, the Act of Appeasement.'

'And she says it too, just like me Gran. He died though and no one knew. But she'll find out,' continued John.

'What does that mean?' asked Simon.

'I'll tell you what it means,' said Sarah. 'Someone in the village has found out about the treasure and is trying to get their hands on it. And I bet I wouldn't have to guess for too long who was mixed up in it either!'

'You mean this Ma Shipton?' suggested John.

'Who better? If she's the descendent of the old witches of Long Compton, the story would have been handed down to her.'

'So the story must have come from this man who saw them turn to stone.'

'Who was he then?'

'Somebody who wasn't in his right mind!' according to Bill Jeffs,' retorted John. 'How much can you believe of a mad man's tale?'

'I'll tell you why he wasn't in his right mind!' exclaimed Sarah. 'Would you feel particularly sane if you'd just seen your friends turned to stone? Don't you see, the only person who could have known about the treasure, apart from the witch, and know roughly where it was hidden, would have to have been one of the King's men!'

John's mouth fell open.

'You mean he was one of the soldiers?'

'Yes.'

'And he told someone about the position of the treasure?'

'I don't think they gave him the chance.'

'They?'

'The witch must have had followers in the village. Remember Bill Jeffs' words? "They found him, but he died and no one knew."'

'Of course!' John let out a low whistle.

'So what happened to the man?' asked Simon in awe.

'Her followers must have found him, and tried to make him talk, and he died.' Sarah paused. The light was fading fast.

'How?' pressed Simon.

Sarah climbed to her feet.

'Witchcraft,' she said.

'Let's get out of here,' said Simon anxiously, as Sarah strode off in the direction of the stones. 'I don't reckon much on this place anymore. Let's get off home!'

John was very ready to agree with him, but something still nagged his thoughts.

'Hey! Sarah!' he shouted. 'The missing stone! you never explained the missing stone!'

Sarah stopped.

John hurried across the centre of the circle towards her.

Simon was making nervous noises to encourage them to return.

'So what's happened to the missing stone?'

'It's obvious isn't it?' said Sarah. 'They've taken it!'

'Why?'

'Because they want to know about the treasure. I don't believe the Shiptons or anyone else in the village have ever known the exact whereabouts of the Place of Appeasement.'

'But Bill Jeffs knew the story. The treasure would be priceless. Why hasn't someone tried to find it before?'

'Because the story would have just been a fairy-tale to most people, like the one about the Stones coming down the hill to drink from the stream. Only the Shiptons would have known the truth. That the Stones were really a King and his army, and that there really was hidden treasure.'

'So what use is the stone to them?'

'I don't know exactly. I've been thinking about it ever since it all clicked together. The only thing I can think of is perhaps there's some clue on it as to the place where the treasure is hidden.'

'You mean some sort of sign?'

'Perhaps.'

'Hey!' cried John, as a thought struck him. 'The arrangement of the Stones! Couldn't that be some kind of message? Perhaps it ...'

Sarah shook her head.

'No, I'd already thought of that. When the witch turned them to stone they would hardly have been likely to shuffle into a special arrangement that would point the way to the treasure, before they became petrified! Anyway old Mother Shipton and her gang must have ruled that out too, otherwise why take just one stone?'

'So who left the clue?' queried John.

'Who do you think? The man who saw them turn!'

'But he died.' John paused. 'Or was killed. I thought you said he didn't have time to tell?'

'He might not have been persuaded to talk, but he might well have left some clue before they caught up with him.'

'Buy why? I thought the place of Appeasement had to be kept a deadly secret?'

'Well, just think. He was probably an ordinary soldier. The thought of all those riches would mean more to him than success in battle, or the anger of the gods. Besides, what use was the Appeasement now? They'd all been turned to stone.'

'So he must have searched around for somewhere to leave a clue, and perhaps hoped that he might escape the fate that had befallen the others, and return some time to retrieve it.'

'What would he have used for a clue?'

'Pretty obvious,' said Sarah. 'He must have put a mark on one of the stones. No prizes for guessing which one!'

John sighed. 'So where do we go from here?'

Sarah shrugged.

'I haven't the foggiest idea. I can't really see us going to the police and telling them our story. We'd spend the rest of our lives in Hatton, beating our heads against padded walls!'

The darkness enveloped them. Only towards the Kingstone did the sky allow a faint chink of disappearing light to illuminate their way back to the road.

Simon was waiting for them.

'For God's sake hurry up!' he squawked. 'I'd just about wet myself with the thought of all them witches and ghosts.' Sarah however felt no terror at all. It was as if she derived some hidden strength and safety from being surrounded by those stone giants, as if she had been a part of the story for a long time.

John hastily agreed with Simon that they should delay their return home no longer. They lit the lamps on their bicycles and wheeled them onto the road.

The Stones in the circle had sunk into darkness but over the road the dying fingers of daylight still cast the Kingstone in sharp silhouette against the sky. Suddenly John wobbled and fell to the road with a crash.

'Bloody hell!' screamed Simon. 'It's them ghosts!'

Sarah leapt from her bicycle and reached John just as he was disentangling himself from his mount.

'What happened?'

'Nothing, nothing at all,' said John hurriedly. 'I just had this idea, that's all.'

'What?'

'You know we were talking about that loony soldier leaving some clue on one of the Stones?'

'Yes, so what?'

'And that was the stone that was missing?'

'Yes, obvious isn't it?' said Sarah impatiently.

Simon had circled back and dismounted and the three children stood in the road-way holding their cycles.

'This soldier, he left a clue on one of the Stones, so that he could come back at some later time, or even perhaps his children, or his children's children, to get the treasure, right?'

'Right,' replied Sarah wearily. 'But we've been through this already.'

'Listen! Do you remember me and my drawing, when we first discovered the stone had gone?'

'Of course, what about it?'

'Do you remember Mr Barnes' explanation? He reckoned I'd got the stones mixed up, and I was quite ready to believe him, and so were most of the class. Lots of the stones look the same.'

'Well?'

'So what about our soldier then? He's already half-way round the bend, having seen his friends turn into stone. How's he going to pick one that he can find again?'

'I get yer,' said Simon, entering the conversation for the first time. 'It's like dogs hiding bones, and not being able to find them again.'

'That's dead right,' said John. 'If you had to find somewhere to leave a clue in a hurry, and be sure that someone other than you would be able to find it, you wouldn't pick a stone that looked like all the rest, would you?'

Sarah gasped.

'The Kingstone!'

John nodded.

The three of them turned to look. As if on cue the Kingstone faded into the darkness as the last light of day fled from the sky.

Eleven

'So they've got the wrong stone!' crowed Simon.

They had halted beside the stile that led over to where the Kingstone stood surrounded by railings.

'What do we do now?'

'I wonder what the chances are of finding a mark on it?' pondered John, glancing dubiously towards the mound.

'Well it makes sense if the rest of our argument is true.'

'How long will it take before Mother Shipton and her helpers discover they've picked the wrong one? That stone's been gone a few weeks now.'

'True,' agreed Sarah.

'I think we should take a closer look at the Kingstone as soon as we can.'

'Oh come on, John, let's get off eh?' Simon pleaded. 'It ain't half creepy here.'

'I thought you were a hard case,' said John not unkindly.

'It's got railings around it,' said Sarah. 'You'd never be able to get close enough to look, not unless you got inside.'

'Couldn't you just climb over?'

'What? In broad daylight! There's always cars passing, or visitors stopping to take photographs. You'd have to come at night.'

'If you climbed over you'd have trouble getting back,' Simon pointed out. 'One of yer could have a piggy-back up, but the last one wouldn't be able to get out.'

'Wasn't there a gate in the railings?' asked Sarah.

Simon, feeling his position as protector somewhat in question, leapt over the stile and ran up the path to the Kingstone. He called back.

'Yeah, it's ever so dark, but I can just see the little gate. It's got a padlock on it though,' he added.

'That's no good then,' said John. 'There'd be no end of trouble if we smashed the lock, and I'm not quite up to James Bond at picking one! Come on Simon, you can come back now!'

There was the distant sound of scuffling.

'What *are* you doing?'

'Hang on!'

Further sounds drifted towards Sarah and John.

Simon eventually reappeared, wiping his hands on his trousers.

'I could get in there I reckon.'

'How?' asked John eagerly.

'Easy,' replied Simon. 'See the railings this side, facing towards the road?'

They nodded.

'That bit of the mound has started to crumble away just by there, where the railings go into the ground. Yer could scrape away the earth around that spot, 'cos it's sort of loose, and yer could slide under the bottom bar of the railing and get out just as easy. See, I just scraped away a bit with my hands.'

He held out two mud-covered palms in evidence.

John was busy working out the details.

'We'd have to come at night, you and me Simon. It's too dangerous for Sarah.'

'If you're coming, I'm coming!' declared Sarah emphatically.

'All right, all right.' said John. 'If you want to risk it you're welcome! We'll need to bring some things with us though.'

'Like what?' asked Simon.

'A small trowel to help clear the earth, a couple of good torches, oh, and something to write on if we find anything.'

'What exactly are we looking for?' asked Simon.

'I don't really know,' replied Sarah. 'Thinking about it, it would have to be some sign that would be preserved from the weather, and not too noticeable to prying eyes. The Kingstone can't have had a railing around it all the time.'

'That's right,' said John. 'Remember it was pulled down the Hill by Bill Jeff's relative. It was probably lying up here completely unguarded in those days.'

'So the mark or clue would probably be carved on it somewhere.'

'That seems sensible.'

'The only thing against it is the way this sort of stone weathers. Remember Mr Barnes telling us how the wind and rain had altered the shapes?'

'That's torn it then, anything marked on it all those years ago would have disappeared by now.'

'Perhaps it's more devious than that. Perhaps it's not carved on it at all.' said John.

'The only way is to look,' said Sarah positively.

'The question is when?'

John looked at Simon who shook his head violently.

'Oh, no! I know what you're thinking. Not likely!'

'But it's got to be tonight. Don't you see, time's getting short, we don't know when they'll realise that they've got the wrong one! We've got to beat them to it!'

'He's right Simon.' Sarah spoke with a new authority. 'It must be done soon.'

'The problem is, how do we get away from home?'

'Oh I don't think that'll be much trouble,' replied Sarah.

'We'll say we're popping over to see Simon about some homework.'

'That's a good idea,' added John. 'Dad doesn't know Simon's parents and they're not on the phone, so I reckon we'll be safe enough for a couple of hours at least.'

'But what do I tell mine?' flustered Simon. Things were getting a little too devious for his liking.

'Easy! You simply tell them that you've popped over to our place!'

'Hah!' Simon grinned briefly, before remembering the purpose of the arrangement. 'I still ain't too keen on coming up here late.'

'It won't be *that* late. About eight o'clock would be best, by the time we've cycled up and had a good look around.'

John looked across to the Kingstone.

'One of us had better stay near the road to signal if anyone is coming,' he pointed out.

'Good idea.'

'Right, see you tonight. Don't forget to bring a good torch. We'll bring the other things.'

They remounted their bicycles and pedalled off down Long Compton Hill.

They met as usual outside the Post Office. Simon was muttering to himself as John and Sarah wheeled silently up to him.

'What's the matter Simon?'

'It's just like the Gestapo getting out of our house. I thought I'd never get out. "Where are you going? Why? Where? What for?" and now my soddin' saddlebag has broken. The catch has gone on it and it won't close properly. I don't want my torch to fall out.'

John fumbled in his pockets and tossed a rounded object across to him. Simon caught it.

'What's this?'

'It's that blue sticky stuff that we have in school, they use it for putting up pictures and displays. I sort of found a ball of it on my desk one day. Roll it out along the edge of the flap and press the other side against it. It'll hold together with a bit of luck.'

'Ta.'

John looked at his watch.

'Come on, let's get it over with.'

They cycled off into the night.

The night was metal grey. Although the children were wrapped in warm anoraks, the cold bit through into their bones, and Sarah had trouble in keeping her teeth from chattering and biting her tongue as she rode along.

Strange by day, the Rollright Stones were imbued with an unearthly magic by night. A strong moon cast their shadows ahead of them as they reached the stile that led to the Kingstone.

'Who's going to keep watch then?' asked John.

Simon rapidly volunteered.

'Right, you stay near the hedge, where we put our bicycles,' ordered John. 'If a car comes along the road flash your torch once. If it's someone on foot keep flashing it on and off until we get back to you.'

Sarah and John blew on their gloved hands to restore their circulation. Simon foraged in his saddlebag for his torch.

'That blue stuff worked OK,' he called.

'What's that?' asked Sarah.

'Just some stuff I gave Simon to mend his saddlebag,' replied John. 'Come on, let's get going.'

Sarah had brought a small red trowel with a wooden handle, and a high-powered torch that she had found in their father's car. John had brought his own smaller torch, which he slipped into the front pocket of his anorak.

'Right,' he hissed. 'Don't forget the signals, Simon.'

They vaulted the stile and sped off down the path. They clambered up to the railings, and briefly shining their torches they saw the scratched earth where Simon had made his excavations that afternoon.

'Let's get digging,' said Sarah. She knelt down and began to gouge out lumps of soil, while John piled it further back with his hands. It was hard work and after a few moments they had both warmed up considerably.

Soon a small pile of earth, slightly larger than a mole-hill, gave enough room for John to squeeze under and reach the inside of the enclosure. The giant stone loomed over him and he tried hard to swallow the feeling of sheer terror that threatened to envelop him, confronted as he was with this monster from the past.

Standing close against it, it seemed far larger than when viewed from the other side of the railings.

After two or three more minutes of digging Sarah slid through and joined him. They turned and looked back to the road. They could just make out the figure of Simon pacing slowly up and down in the moonlight.

Across the road the larch trees whispered to the Circle.

The Kingstone gleamed.

'It's like being lit up by a searchlight,' said John, as he edged his way to the side of the stone furthest away from the road.

Sarah had got down on her hands and knees and was examining small areas of stone. Gradually she worked her way around the base and back again. John followed suit.

'Let's move up and look a little higher,' suggested Sarah.

Just as she spoke a torch beam flashed out from the hedge.

'Down!' hissed John and grabbed Sarah by the sleeve of her anorak.

They fell into a heap at the foot of the stone and waited with their hearts thumping in their throats. Across the headland a car's headlights cut the darkness. Nearer and nearer they came, and now they could hear the sound of its engine as it slowed down.

Sarah and John held their breath.

The car slowed almost to a standstill at the lay-by, and then, just as swiftly, it accelerated away.

'Phew!' breathed Sarah. She clambered up and dusted some mud off her jeans.

'Let's get on with it.'

There were no more warnings from Simon and after three quarters of an hour of intensive searching, their eyes bleary with the efforts of squinting into the torch-light, they were ready to accept defeat.

'What about nearer the top?' asked Sarah. 'We've looked just about everywhere else!'

'But it wouldn't have been that high up would it?' said John. 'Not if he had to do it on his own and in a hurry.'

'Wait a minute,' said Sarah, as a thought struck her. 'It's been moved at least once, remember Bill Jeffs' story? It might well have been at a lower level before. Come on! Get up on my shoulders. I'm bigger than you. Get up and have a quick look at the top part!'

John struggled into an ungainly piggy-back position and tried to maintain a precarious hold on both torch and stone. Sarah wobbled dangerously.

'Hold still!' complained John.

He searched the top-most part of the Kingstone with care.

Nothing.

'There's nothing up here!' he muttered, and was about to relieve Sarah of his weight when he noticed a small crevice near the fold of the rock at the top of the stone. It was at an angle that would make it invisible from ground level.

'Oughh!'

He rolled to the ground, as Sarah's legs finally gave way beneath her.

He sat up.

'What did you say these stones were made of?'

'Oolitic limestone.'

'That's right, Simon's Who-licked-it limestone. That means it's full of holes doesn't it?'

'Yes,' replied Sarah 'But there doesn't seem to be many on the Kingstone, not like the smaller ones in the Circle.'

'Oh there's one on this all right,' said John. 'I've just caught sight of it. You can't see it from down here.'

Sarah clutched at him in the darkness.

'How big is it?'

'Quite a few inches I'd say.'

'Could that be it?'

'I don't know. I can't see how we can find out either. In this light we'd never be able to see anything, and we can't come back in the daylight and look, can we?'

'What sort of message could there possibly be inside a hole anyway?' said Sarah. 'You can't stick a note in there and expect it to last a thousand years.'

'I've got it!' cried John. 'It's probably carved into the rock on the side of the hole. It would be safe there, not likely to be noticed, and unharmed by the weather.'

Sarah's eyes gleamed in the darkness.

'I bet you're right. But how on earth can we tell?'

John was slithering through the hole beneath the railings.

'Where are you going? Hey! Don't leave me here!' shouted Sarah.

'Don't panic. I'll be back in a minute. I've got to get something off Simon. I've had an idea!' John's voice faded as he scrambled headlong down the path.

Alone, Sarah became increasingly aware of her surroundings. It was as if some enormous latent power lay within the Kingstone, touching her mind. Somehow she did not feel afraid. She felt her whole being swept along waves of force, images running through her mind like characters in a speeded-up old film. Dark looming figures that froze into stillness, and a girl with *her* face standing against the headland. The girl turned and a dark shape in the corner of her eye dissolved into spreading branch-like shapes. Her head began to reel and the next thing she knew was the Kingstone gleaming coldly in the moonlight and John struggling beneath the railings.

'Didn't take long, did I?' John clambered beside her clutching a ball of blue adhesive plaster.

'Hey! Are you OK?'

'Just a bit faint with excitement,' whispered Sarah. Thank goodness he'd come back. She'd been sure she had fainted or something. That strange vision. What had it meant?

'I got this.'

He proffered the ball to Sarah who gazed at it blankly.

'What on earth is it?'

'Give me a lift up again and I'll show you. If there's anything worth knowing about inside the stone, this will find it.'

'I don't get you.'

'If there's some carving or any mark that sticks out on the inside of that hole, this will take an impression of it,' John explained. 'Now come on, lift me up so that I can get inside.'

As he spoke he kneaded the ball like putty in his hands, finally he smoothed the surface until it was clear of blemishes.

'Right, up we go!'

Sarah tensed her back as John clambered onto her shoulders. Searching frantically for a hold he found the crevice and inserted his fingers. He rapidly withdrew them. If the markings were at all weather-worn they may well prove too fragile to withstand his fingers poking around inside. He couldn't risk destroying anything. He groped with his free hand and squeezed the adhesive into the hole. Luckily the wedge was large enough to fill the crevice. He squeezed it and pressed hard against his palm to ensure that any mark would 'bite'.

'Found anything?' called Sarah.

'Don't know till I get down.'

Delicately he lifted the flattened edges of the filling away from the outer stone face, and, almost not daring to breath, he carefully eased out the flattened plaster and held it gently away from his body.

'Right-oh! Let me down!'

He landed lightly this time, still holding his arm out stiffly to protect the piece of adhesive putty.

Sarah huddled against him and shone the torch into his hand. John carefully turned over the blue wedge and they gazed in wonder as the cold beam of light illuminated the shadows and curves that were etched into the smooth surface.

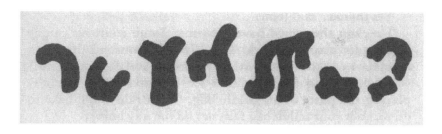

They looked at one another. Fear mingled with the joy of their discovery. Sarah looked at it, as if she had known a thousand years before that they would find it there.

'That's it!' said John hoarsely. 'The sign. It did exist! Everything we said is true! But what does it mean?'

'It's the wrong way round,' said Sarah. 'When we get home we'll have to trace it in the mirror.'

'Couldn't we soak it in ink and do a print of it?'

'No. As soon as you pressed the marks would disappear. The putty's too soft.'

'You're right,' said John softly. 'Now let's get away from here double quick!'

Carefully, as if carrying a great weight, John edged his way around the Kingstone until he reached the gap. Sarah slipped through first, and gingerly John transferred the precious material into Sarah's hands. Quickly he followed her through the hole and hurriedly scooped back some of the earth against the railing.

'They'll just reckon on it being moles I hope,' he said.

They walked as if on thin ice until they reached the stile where Simon was waiting.

'Cor, I'm glad to see you,' said Simon vehemently. 'It's bloody freezin' up here. Did yer find anything?'

'Yes. I think we've got it,' gasped Sarah.

'Let's have a look!' said Simon eagerly, craning his neck towards John's outstretched hand.

'Keep clear, Simon,' warned John. 'We've got to take care not to touch it until we get back and sketch it in a mirror.'

'Eh?' Simon looked perplexed.

'I'll explain on the way home, Simon,' said Sarah.

'OK.. Hey did you see my signal?'

'Yes thanks,' said John.

'I reckon they must have seen me. Some courting couple looking for a spot to park. They slowed down and then they must have caught sight of me by the hedge and they drove off.'

'Well, as long as they didn't see us,' said John, carefully placing the putty in his saddle bag. 'I'm afraid you'll have to do without your saddlebag fastener on the way home.'

'It don't matter.' Simon was just thankful to be going back.

Back at home John and Sarah transferred the imprint to John's bedroom. Just before they went to bed John positioned the putty in front of his mirror and, with infinite patience, he traced every curve and squiggle that was reflected onto his piece of paper. Sarah leaned over to examine the result.

It made as little sense as the mirror writing.

Later that night John lay in bed going over in his mind the strange shapes that he had drawn. What did it mean?

In the next bedroom Sarah groaned in her sleep as she saw once again the girl with her face, surrounded by dark and mysterious figures.

Twelve

Extract from the local newspaper dated Tuesday 28th November 1978:

ROLLRIGHT STONE MYSTERY
KINGSTONE VANISHES

Long Compton, Sunday.

Oxfordshire and Warwickshire police are today investigating the mysterious disappearance of the largest of the Rollright Stones, a megalithic circle on the Oxfordshire border near the village of Long Compton.

The stone circle is said to rank in importance with Stonehenge and Avebury, and has long been associated with outbreaks of witchcraft in the area.

The missing stone, measuring almost eight feet by six feet, and weighing in the region of several tons, stood apart from the main circle in a nearby field.

The disappearance was discovered by Mrs Alison Squire of Little Rollright, who was driving along the road that passes the stones at seven o'clock on Sunday morning, on her way to Stratford.

'I usually glance at them as I pass,' she told our reporter, 'and you can imagine my surprise when I couldn't see the Kingstone for love nor money!'

Mrs Squire stopped her car and went to investigate. She found the railings surrounding the Kingstone bent and twisted out of recognition, a trail of gouged earth leading to the roadway, seeming to suggest that a massive object had been dragged along the ground. The stile and hedge leading onto the road had also been destroyed.

A police spokesman said last night that all the evidence pointed to the Kingstone having been removed by an organised gang using heavy earth-moving equipment, and inquiries were continuing in this direction. 'I feel sure' he concluded 'that this outrage was the work of some irresponsible pranksters intent on playing a rather bizarre practical joke, rather than the work of a witches' coven.'

In recent years however police have been called many times to the Circle to break up gatherings of latter-day witches, particularly at Halloween and other occult occasions on the calendar. Remains of 'witch-fires' can easily be found today in the centre of the main ring of stones.

Legend tells that the missing stone was once a pagan King who was transformed together with his army, by a Long Compton witch, for daring to attempt to become the King of England.

A representative of the owners has requested all visitors to try and avoid this particular monument for the next few days in order that police investigations may continue unhampered, and so that certain temporary repairs can be made.

Return of the Warwickshire Witches? Feature article on page 15.

Thirteen

The three figures stood alone in the playground of the school. It was as yet far too early for either the staff or any other children to have arrived. Only the caretaker was busy, polishing the windows of the staff room, as the group huddled in deep conversation.

Sarah was clutching a copy of the morning newspaper. Suddenly the events had been transformed into a deadly serious matter. The thought of the police and newspapers made them shiver at the enormity of the act that had taken place.

'Look,' said John, 'We've just got to keep calm. I think our best bet is to go to the police.'

'Bloody hell, not likely!' exclaimed Simon. 'Not after this little lot! What do we tell them? "Oh, by the way we were climbing around inside the Kingstone railings last night, but we don't know anything about it disappearing, honest!"'

'Don't be daft Simon. How could we have carried a thing that size away?' said Sarah.

'He's right though,' John pointed out. 'If we just gave them a hint that we'd been near there on Saturday night they'd have us locked away in no time! Anyway, what could we tell them that would be of any help? Perhaps it *was* just someone playing a practical joke.'

Sarah snorted.

'You know as well as I do what happened. Mother Shipton and her friends have discovered their mistake. They've taken the Kingstone for themselves. We weren't a day too soon in carrying out our search.'

At the mention of Saturday night's adventure their minds flew to the strange hieroglyphics that they had found. Simon had gone round to John and Sarah's house the following morning and they had been just as mystified by the corrected version as the original imprint.

'Had any more ideas about those marks?' asked Simon.

'No,' replied Sarah, pushing the newspaper into her pocket. 'I suppose it's some sort of code, but heaven knows if we'll ever be able to work it out.'

'We still haven't decided what we should do about the missing Kingstone,' said John.

Sarah thought for several moments.

The playground began to fill with children.

'I think we ought to let sleeping dogs lie for the moment,' she said. 'Let's see if we can work out anything from the imprint. Besides, we can't just go to the police and tell them to look in Mother Shipton's cottage for it, they're hardly going to believe that an old lady of sixty or seventy is going to have a desperate urge to steal seven tons of limestone.'

'Perhaps she's going to make a rockery,' said Simon, deadpan.

'Sometimes I wonder just how much you take in,' said Sarah disparagingly.

The bell rang.

'How about telling Mr Barnes?' said John as they pushed their way into the building. 'Perhaps he might be able to help.'

'Oh I don't know,' replied Sarah. 'He'll have seen the headline in the paper and put two and two together about our interfering.'

'Don't let's tell him that bit then,' said John. 'Let's just tell him about the witches. I bet he'd be pleased to know we've done all this work on our own.'

'OK.'

After assembly the children filed out of the Hall and into their home bays. Mr Barnes was taking the register, and, as usual, once this was completed, he put aside ten minutes for the children to discuss anything of interest that had occurred during the weekend.

'Mr Barnes! What do you think of the Stone going missing?' asked one of the children.

Mr Barnes frowned. 'What stone's going missing?' he queried. 'The one John was telling us about the other week?'

'Haven't you seen the paper?' chorused several of the class in unison. 'The Rollright Stones! The Kingstone's disappeared!'

'Very funny,' retorted Mr Barnes. 'Now seriously, hasn't anyone got any proper news to tell?'

Sarah rummaged in her pocket.

'Here you are, Mr Barnes!'

He took the paper from her hand and read quickly.

'What do you make of that Mr Barnes?' they cried.

'Students!' he exclaimed. Mr Barnes was noted for his low opinion of students and practical jokers. 'Just the sort of thing students would do. I expect it's a rag-day stunt or some such nonsense.'

'Mr Barnes?'

'Yes, John?'

'Remember when we told you about our missing stone?'

'Well?'

'We've been doing ever such a lot of follow up work on it, haven't we Sarah?' Sarah nodded in confirmation.

'And we found out all sorts of things about Long Compton village.'

'Such as?'

Mr Barnes leaned closer to catch John's words above the general discussion that was going on around the class. Everyone was airing their pet theory as to the Kingstone's disappearance. Favourite was Stuart Crawford's suggestion that flying saucers had made off with it in the belief that it was representative of planet Earth's highest form of intelligence.

'Sarah and Simon and me went back there a few times and found out all about the witches and how it wasn't just a story from long ago, and there's an old man there who knew all these fantastic tales about his great great great grandfather being cursed by a witch, and there was a murder there a hundred years ago when a farm labourer killed a witch named ...'

'Good, good. Very interesting John. I'm pleased that you've gone into it a little more deeply. However, you don't want to pay too much attention to all the old stories you hear. Most villages have an old man who hasn't got anything better to do than to make up stories to frighten youngsters.'

Mr Barnes stood up.

'Now listen carefully. We'll be bringing our present project to an end today.'

'Aw, but Mr Barnes, couldn't we follow up the news about the missing Kingstone?'

'No, I'm afraid not.' replied Mr Barnes. 'We've spent far longer than we should on it already. I'll collect your folders in this morning while you're looking up information on our new topic. Now it's time we got down to some Maths.'

The group broke up and work began.

At home time Sarah, John and Simon met briefly.

'He wasn't much interested in our story was he?' said John sadly.

'Huh! Teachers!' snorted Sarah. 'They never listen when you've got something to tell *them*.'

'I'd like to have a look at what's happened up at the Circle,' said John. 'The only trouble is, it's too dark after school to see anything.'

Sarah nodded in agreement. 'If you must go, we'd best leave it till the weekend, besides it said in the paper that people should keep away.'

'Oh I expect all the fuss will be over by the weekend. Besides, we're not just anybody are we? We've got a good reason for going. It's not as if we were just sight-seers. Let's go on Saturday morning then and see what happens.'

John collected his anorak from his peg. He plunged his hands into the pockets and extracted a piece of paper.

'Here, I did another copy for you, Simon. Perhaps you might have some bright ideas during the week.'

'Thanks,' said Simon. 'But I think you'd best give it to your sister, she's cleverer than I am at that sort of thing.'

John handed it to Sarah.

'Thanks, but I can't make head or tail of it either, Simon!'

They walked to the bicycle shed, collected their bikes and rode home.

Fourteen

The first Saturday in December was cold and clear. The road into Long Compton was hardened with frost and the children rode carefully to avoid puddles of water that had turned to ice during the night.

After a week of frustration at not being able to decipher the print they decided to confide in the only other person they felt might have an interest in the matter: Dave Coulbeck.

Accordingly, they cycled up to the entrance of Clark's Lane and leaned their bicycles against the fence. They trooped up to his door and rang the bell.

'Hello! I was wondering when I'd clap eyes on you again!'

'Hello,' they chorused. 'Would you mind if we came in?'

A frosty wind tugged at their clothing.

'No, no, come on in. Take your coats off. I'll put the kettle on. I expect you wouldn't say no to that would you?'

He ushered them into the kitchen.

'Well, you've got plenty to exercise your imaginations on now all right,' he said. 'What with the Kingstone disappearing like it has.'

'That's what we wanted to talk to you about,' said Sarah urgently.

'Oh?'

He pottered around the kitchen spooning coffee into thick earthenware mugs and filling up the kettle.

'You'd best be telling me all about it then.'

The kettle boiled, and he poured the scalding water into the mugs.

Picking up two in each hand he led the way into the living room.

'The wife's taken the baby down into the village to do some shopping,' he said. 'So we've got the place to ourselves for the next hour or so.'

They warmed their hands against the mugs and inhaled the smell of fresh coffee. Gradually their tale was unfolded and Dave put down his mug and listened with rapt concentration as they explained their find in the crevice of the Kingstone.

'I knew there was summat fishy about that place,' said Dave when they had done. 'Old Mother Shipton eh? That explains a few things.'

'How do you mean?'

'All the comings and goings late at night recently. I've half a mind to believe you.'

'But it is true,' cried Sarah. 'How else do you explain what has happened to the Kingstone?'

'You've got a point there, at that,' agreed Dave.

'Have you been up to the Circle since the disappearance?' asked John.

'No I haven't,' Dave shook his head. 'I was meaning to go up there this afternoon and have a look around out of interest. I hear there's been no end of people up there since it got in the papers.'

'Aren't you going up there then?'

Dave shook his head again.

'Don't see how I'll manage it today. I've got to get over to Warwick after lunch to have the old car MOT'd otherwise I'll be off the road. Maybe I'll pop up there tomorrow.'

Sarah was hunting inside the front pocket of her anorak.

At last she located the scrap of paper that John had given her.

'Here you are, this is a copy of the print we took. I'm afraid we're absolutely stumped by it. I suppose it's some sort of code.'

'Do you mind if I hang on to it?' Dave asked.

'No, keep it. John's got another copy in his pocket. But whatever you do don't go handing it over to Mother Shipton!'

Dave took out his wallet and carefully placed the paper inside it.

'Aye, her,' he mused. 'What shall we do about her? Have you considered going to the police? They'd be your best bet you know.'

Sarah explained the reasons for their decision to leave well alone, and eventually Dave agreed that it was probably the best course for the time being.

'We're just on our way to the Circle to have a look around,' said John as they got up to go.

'Sorry I haven't been much help to you,' said Dave as they headed towards the door. 'It'll take some digesting though will all this. I wonder why they've never looked for a sign before?'

'Has Mother Shipton got any relatives? You know, brothers, sisters, children?'

Dave thought carefully.

'None that I know about.'

'I wonder,' murmured Sarah. 'I wonder if that's the reason behind the search. If the story had been passed down from generation to generation perhaps she was afraid it would end with her. Perhaps she wants to do something before her line dies out completely.'

'Couldn't she just tell someone else?' suggested Dave.

'Some of her visitors seem to know about it, Bill Jeffs for one!'

'Don't forget,' laughed John, 'she's supposed to be a witch!'

They all laughed at John's joke. All except Sarah.

They trailed from Dave's house and glanced back down the Lane, at the little cottage nestling at the far end. By unspoken agreement they had not passed the door since their discoveries. In fact they had never knowingly caught sight of Mother Shipton.

'Cheerio then, thanks for the coffee and the help,' said John.

'I've been no help so far,' said Dave, his brow still wrinkled in thought. 'But leave things with me and I'll see if I can work anything out. Why don't you call in tomorrow if you're passing this way. I might have come up with something by then.'

'I feel better just having talked to you about it,' said Sarah with feeling. And in truth the three of them made their way up the Hill with lighter hearts than they had had for many a long day.

Fifteen

The door opened and she examined the face that stood before her.

'Come.'

The door closed.

'I told you I would send when the time was right,' her voice was without feeling. Cold and distant.

'I had to come Mother,' his voice trembled slightly.

'Well get it over then, I have no time to waste, as well you should know!'

'These children ...'

'Children! Again!'

'Aye, meddlers. They've been finding out a little too much. I'm sure they know. I'm afeared of what they could do! If they went to the police and told half, particularly after the other night ...'

His voice trailed away to silence as he became aware of the terrible power in her eyes. At last she spoke.

'You crawling maggot! Call yourself a man? What harm can come to you from *children* when you have seen the Power that we command? What of their idle tales? They would be dismissed as the imaginings of youthful minds! You think the police would enter here and search for missing stones? And think you not that the Old Ways could deal with them if need be?'

Her visitor stammered.

'No Mother. But just in case, shouldn't something be done?'

She turned away and a silence fell in the old room.

'It is not the children I fear so much as the faithlessness of those that doubt my powers,' she snarled. 'For that reason alone I make it my concern.'

'Whatever you say Mother,' snivelled the man.

'It will not be the first time that the Old Ways have been threatened by interfering minds,' she muttered.

'Know this, my friend. She that lies in the church doorway was once of flesh and blood. That is no carved statue done to honour the soul of a young girl tragically carried to her rest. Rather it is the mark of supreme vengeance on one who sought to threaten the Power that the Shiptons have held since time immemorial. That meddler rests in stone, and she came to that end through obstruction of our Powers.'

'I never knew! But they say it is of Saint Augustine!'

She gave a hollow laugh.

'No! A meddler. One who paid the price. Now for the peace of mind of those whose weakness may yet betray our aims, so shall those children be dealt with! Now go! And leave me to my workings!'

The door opened and he left, stumbling blindly into the road.

She closed the door and returned to the ancient room. The darkness closed around her, for since the previous week the curtains had remained closed both day and night.

On the wooden table lay the first stone, resting on its cloth. Behind it lay the wall of the cottage. On closer examination no single blocks of stone were visible. The wall was one solid mass, curved and twisted to the roof. Its summit vanishing into the wooden beams that lined the ceiling.

She stepped up to the wall and laid her hand against it. The Kingstone sweated in the cloying atmosphere of its prison.

'Soon, oh, very soon, you shall talk with us!' she crooned.

'But first the small matter of our meddling friends.'

She had found no need to admit to the Watcher that her disquiet lay not with the lack of faith in her helpers, but in the children.

She knew now from whence the force derived that rendered her magic half-complete.

The girl.

Once, at the beginning, there had also been a girl.

In those days the Earth Mother had been worshipped throughout the land. But the temptation to use the powers that were given to those who dedicated their lives to Wicca for their own ends had led the Shiptons to corruption. Lust and greed for power had led them from the True Religion. Their worship had become a travesty of the beauty and wonder of the Elder Way and their dealings had turned towards the darker forces of the world.

It was then that the girl had come.

Pure and beautiful.

She had held the true power of Wicca.

It was to the Shipton of that time she came, to give counsel and to bring a warning, but the Shipton paid no heed, for she planned that very night to provide the greatest challenge for her new found evil powers. The transformation of an entire army and the possession of untold riches.

They met upon the headland that night, and as the Shipton had wrought her deed the girl had used her powers also. The Shipton changed before her eyes into an eldern tree. And that would have been an end, but the rest of Shipton's brood had observed these things and emboldened by their hideous new found strength, gained on surety of their souls, they overwhelmed her. But before she had been commuted to her basic clay the girl had sworn upon the name of the Earth Mother that she would return.

The girl.

The true Witch of Rollright.

She now rested in stone in Long Compton Church.

And now another had come. Did she too have the Power? The true Power of Wicca? But now that her identity was known her disposal could soon be accomplished! Her two friends also, for although no man could hold the Power, the boys too could no longer be suffered to live.

Tonight.

She would speak the Words tonight.

Arrangements must be made.

Sixteen

Dave Coulbeck reversed his old blue Volkswagen into Clark's Lane and pulled out onto the main road. The engine rattled as he accelerated out of the village and headed in the direction of Warwick. It was late morning and he hoped that he could get his MOT test completed, pick up some odd items of shopping, and be back in time for a late lunch. Maybe he would be able to take a look at the Circle that afternoon after all.

He pondered over the story that the children had told. How much of it was childish fantasy? Yet it explained many of the strange happenings that had occurred recently. He decided to make some inquiries of his own in Warwick while he waited for his car.

The roads were quiet and he made good time. After leaving his car at the garage he set off into the town. Searching in his pocket for the scrap of paper that Sarah had given him, he strode purposefully through the Butts and down Cape Street towards a driveway sheltered by bushes that lay just behind the police station. The notice near the entrance read:

COUNTY RECORDS OFFICE

Dave stepped up the driveway and found himself in the courtyard of an old Priory. Ahead of him lay a flight of steps that led to a small bridge of wooden planks and an entrance hall containing glass display cabinets. He had remembered this place and something at the back of his mind told him that the solution to his problem might lie within the vast collection of material concerning the County that was stored there.

He had visited the Office once before, when he had been searching out the rights-of-way near to his house, and the staff had proved most helpful. He had also been impressed with their encyclopaedic knowledge of local history. It was here that he had first become interested in the legends of the village, and had discovered the basis of many of the stories he had later heard from Bill Jeffs and the children.

He pushed through the door and strolled into the main Reading Room. It was quite crowded inside. Several people were sitting at desks consulting large documents or maps, and earnestly scribbling in note-books. There was an air of scholarly research as people moved reverently about the room carrying their precious finds. A subdued hum of conversation filled the place as visitors consulted with experts.

A tall grey-haired man caught Dave's eye and immediately came over to him.

'Can I help you at all?'

'Er, yes.' replied Dave. 'I was wondering how I'd set about finding the names of villages or places in Warwickshire going back at least a thousand years?'

'That should be easy enough,' said the Archivist, heading towards a set of shelves halfway down the room. He stopped and scanned the titles and reached out to extract an old book bound in blue leather.

'Place Names of Warwickshire,' he said. 'If that's no help come back and we'll have another look.'

Dave thanked him and carried the volume to a large desk.

He made himself comfortable. This was likely to take some time. He studied the scrap of paper that Sarah had given him and had come to the conclusion that the markings were not in any code. If Sarah's story was true, then the poor beggar who had made the marks would have been in no condition, or have had the time, to compose a cipher. It was funny that the children hadn't thought of that. What lay inside the Kingstone must be simply the hurried scratching of the place-name where the Act of Appeasement had been carried out. However the names of the places would have changed many times since that mark had been made. Luckily the style of lettering used was not too different from that found today. He looked at the thick book that lay on the desk before him. It was certainly going to take some time. But perhaps he could narrow things down a little. He consulted the scrap of paper again. The first letter of the word most resembled a 'C' or an 'O'. He idly pencilled in a 'C'. There was obviously an 'M', you could tell by the extra down stroke. And a 'B' or was it an 'H'? The letter 'R' was more certain. 'COMHRUO'? 'OCMBRUC'? Best to begin with the letter 'C' and keep his fingers crossed that he was on the right track.

He turned to the first few pages 'C', 'C', 'C'....

He delved deeper into the book, glancing along columns of names and dates, each changing and reforming before his eyes, letters and words melting in a dance of time. The hypnotic nature of his task began to assert itself and the combination of whispered voices and warm surroundings caused him to doze off for split seconds at a time as he ploughed onward through the lines of print. Suddenly his eyes were arrested by an entry on page 252.

Combrook.
Cumbroc (e) 1217 CIR
1227 Ch. 1231 1233 C1
Pat – brok 1228, 1304 Ass.
1316 FA 1656 Dugdale
Combroke 1279 Nott 1325
1327 Pat – brocke 1591
'Valleybrook' v cumb.
The reference is to the stream which flows down the combe of Compton Verney and passes the village of Combrook.

He scanned the page once more.
CUMBROC! CUMBROC!
He read it through again, anxious to confirm his first impression. His pencil sketched in the missing portions of the letters.
The result was clear.

The letters fitted!
'Reference to a stream which flows down the combe of Compton Verney and passes the village of Combrook.'
Water.
What had Sarah said? 'The King would throw all his treasure into a lake or stretch of water as a gift to the gods to ensure success in battle.'
But where was Combrook? He had never heard of it.
He hurried across to the Archivist who was immersed in conversation with a woman trying to trace her family tree.

'Come on, come on!' Dave willed her to finish talking but she seemed intent on reciting her entire family history. After what seemed an age she finished and the Archivist turned to him.

'Did you find what you were looking for?'

'Yes, thanks,' said Dave. 'Just one more thing, I was wondering if you know where a place called Combrook was exactly?'

The Archivist barely paused for thought.

'Between Wellesbourne and Kineton,' he replied softly.

'Follow the main Banbury road, it's a right turn, just after you pass Compton Verney.'

'You wouldn't happen to know if there's a stretch of water nearby?' queried Dave.

'Yes, of course. Combrook Lake. It leads from Compton Verney. Quite large, privately owned, but there's a footpath most of the way around it I believe.'

'Thanks. Thank you very much,' gasped Dave, and incurred the Archivist's displeasure by making a speedy exit, the doors swinging wildly behind him.

He had to find the children and tell them. CUMBROC-COMBROOK! The lake! The question was, what did they do about it now?

There was a carnival air about the Rollrights as the children arrived on the scene. Surrounding the area of the missing Kingstone were rows and rows of red and white plastic strips usually found marking off road works. Gathered as close to these as possible was a crowd of fifty or so onlookers. In the lay-by opposite the Kingstone a police panda car was parked amongst the other vehicles, and a harassed constable was trying to maintain order amongst the sight-seers.

'Keep clear of the markers please!' he appealed every few minutes, but the curious edged closer to examine with relish the very spot from where the Kingstone had been spirited away.

A buzz of conversation filled the air as strangers exchanged opinions as to its removal.

The children parked their bicycles in the lay-by and hurried across the road towards the crowd. There was no longer any need to climb over the stile. Both it and the hedge had been totally destroyed.

'God,' breathed Sarah. 'They must have dragged it across the field and into the road in one go! Look at those markings along the ground!'

They followed the muddy path towards the gaping hole that was all that now remained of the Kingstone. It reminded John of an empty gum after a tooth had been extracted. They edged towards the barrier but the crowd was too dense.

'Wonder what they find to gawk at all this time,' said Simon. 'It's just a hole, nothing else to them.'

'Ah,' replied Sarah, 'it's the idea of witchcraft. They could make a goldmine up here now if they wanted to.'

'Let's go back,' said John. 'It's all been trampled up around the spot where the Kingstone used to be. There's nothing more to be gained by hanging around.'

'There's one thing about it,' whispered Sarah confidentially. 'At least there's no sign of our little tunnelling effort. Just look at the state of those railings. I reckon they must have had a bulldozer up here to shift things like that.'

'That's funny,' said John. 'Have you noticed along the pathway, there's no sign of any track at all? I thought it said in the newspaper that the police had proved that it had been done with mechanical diggers.'

Sarah glanced at the scar that had been traced across the ground.

'What probably happened was that they dragged it backwards to the road and the weight of the Kingstone rubbed out any tracks that they made.'

'I suppose that's it,' said John.

'Here!' Simon was kneeling near the hedge.

'What is it Simon?'

'Have yer seen the ground just by here?'

Sarah and John ambled over to where Simon was kneeling.

'It ain't half funny.'

They knelt down beside him. He was holding a handful of muddy earth that had been hardened by frost. It was charred and scorched, and as he crumbled it in his hand, it left a sooty deposit.

Sarah and John picked up a handful and did the same. Again, a black mark remained on their fingers.

'I've never seen anything like that before,' said Simon.

'Perhaps the police burnt some of the hedge when they were tidying up,' said John. He looked around for signs of burnt-out branches or a pile of wood-ash. There was nothing.

'I don't think it's that at all,' said Simon. 'You look along the trail that the rock made, it's the same all the way along, all blackened around the edges of the furrow.'

'It's almost as if the Kingstone had burnt a path to the road,' said Sarah.

The Power of Earth, Water, Air and *Fire*. Sarah kept the thought to herself. How often the old elements of magic had figured in their discoveries! She was intensely aware of the power that had been released upon this place. She knew too that the power was evil, and that somehow she was able to pick up its vibrations. Her mind tottered as she felt the raw surge of magic try to overcome her. It was the first time she had openly admitted to herself her awareness of these unseen things. Her head began to spin and the scene seemed to fade from her. She blinked her eyes, the sky was dark, and yet in the darkness she saw once again the girl with her face. She seemed to radiate a gentle white light, but gradually darkness began to surround her.

The sky brightened again and the boys' voices returned.

'Ain't that Bill Jeffs?' exclaimed Simon.

'Where?' snapped John, spinning around to examine the crowd.

'Over there, by the woman in the red anorak!'

John saw a bent figure stumble around the barriers.

'Yes, that's him all right. I wonder why he's risked coming up here? He wouldn't be so cocky if he knew what we'd discovered!'

A hand reached out and grasped John's shoulder.

He jumped.

'Hello John. Hello Sarah, Simon!' It was Mr Barnes. He nodded to each of the children. 'What are you three doing up here? More investigating?' he grinned.

'We just thought we'd come up and have a look,' said John.

'That was just what I thought too!' he replied. 'I hadn't heard about it until I read your newspaper cutting, and as we've done such a lot of work on it in school I couldn't miss the chance of coming up to see for myself.'

'There's not much left to see is there?' said Sarah sadly.

'Whoever took it made a terrible mess.'

'They did that all right,' agreed Mr Barnes. 'I wonder if they've caught those students yet?'

'Students, what students?' asked Simon dimly.

'From some college or other! Sort of trick you play when you're away from home! They ought to have brought it back by now, owned up, paid for the repairs to the fence and hedge, and no more harm done.'

'But we know ....' Simon's voice was silenced by the look in Sarah's eyes.

'Know what?' asked Mr Barnes.

'Er, we know that already. You told us on Monday,' stammered Simon. Sarah breathed again. Once more Simon had proved that his wits were sharpest in a crisis, albeit one of his own making.

She hadn't wanted Simon to tell Mr Barnes. He had had his chance on Monday and hadn't listened to them then. She didn't want to be made fun of again. Time enough to tell him when they gathered all the evidence, but until they solved the riddle of the print and proved Mother Shipton was indeed involved there was little point in involving anyone else. It had been a hard enough job to convince Dave Coulbeck, she felt it would be even harder to convince Mr Barnes.

'I think we'll be heading home,' said John presently.

'We've seen everything really. See you on Monday, Mr Barnes.'

'I'll walk back with you,' said Mr Barnes. 'It's time I was getting home as well.'

Together they threaded their way through the ruts of frozen mud flung up by the Kingstone's departure.

'People aren't very observant,' thought John sourly. 'Those scorch marks stand out a mile.'

They reached the lay-by where they had left their bicycles.

'Well, cheerio, see you next week.' Mr Barnes strolled towards his car. The children turned to pick up their bicycles.

'That's funny. I could have sworn this was where we left them,' said John, gazing along the fence. 'But they're not here.'

Sarah looked at the spot where they had been left.

'They *were* here,' she said. 'Look, you can see the tyre marks in the mud.'

Simon searched down the row of parked cars in case someone had moved them to allow a car to park. He returned shaking his head.

'Stones ain't the only bloody things to go missing up here,' he exclaimed angrily.

'But where would they have gone?'

'Someone must have stolen them!'

'Who on earth would want *three* bicycles?'

91

'Three kids.' said John. 'I bet there's no end of kids been up there this afternoon. 'I bet they took them off for a ride. Perhaps they'll bring them back in a minute.'

'Use your sense,' said Sarah. 'No one's going to risk pinching three bikes in one go. Let's hurry up and tell Mr Barnes about it. He hasn't gone yet.'

They raced down to his car.

Mr Barnes sat in the front seat drinking coffee from a flask.

'Mr Barnes! Mr Barnes! We've had our bikes nicked! Yer didn't see anybody take them did yer?' asked Simon in a rush.

Mr Barnes carefully put down his flask.

'Your bicycles? Gone? When?'

'Now! Just this minute. While we were talking to you!'

'Where did you leave them?'

'Up the road, against the fence at the top of the lay-by!'

'Did you see anyone around there when you came in?'

Mr Barnes paused to think.

'Now that you mention it, I did. An old man I think it was, wearing a cloth cap.'

'Bill Jeffs! I knew it!' gasped John.

Mr Barnes glanced at him.

'You know him then?'

'Yes, er, well, it might be someone we met when we were asking about the stones.'

'How could he have stolen three bikes though?' interrupted Simon. 'He couldn't ride em all!'

'I think the best thing for us to do is to go down to the police station in the village,' said Mr Barnes. 'It's just at the bottom of the hill, on the corner. I'll give you a lift.'

'Hey thanks!'

He leaned over and lifted the locking mechanism on the passenger doors and Sarah climbed into the front seat while John and Simon clambered into the back. Mr Barnes fastened the top of his flask, adjusted his seat belt and started the engine. The car swerved out of the lay-by and executed a fast three point turn in the road. Mr Barnes accelerated away rapidly.

'You never know, if we step on it we may be able to catch up with the culprits!'

John and Simon sank back into their seats as the car picked up speed. It braked sharply at the crossroads and turned down Long Compton Hill.

'Me Dad'll murder me if I've lost that bike,' said Simon. 'I only had it for me birthday.'

'Don't worry,' Mr Barnes assured him. 'I'm positive the police will be able to help.'

'It's very good of you bother,' said Sarah politely. 'We could have just mentioned it to the policeman on duty up there if we'd thought.'

'The police-station will be best,' said Mr Barnes. 'More official.'

As the car sped to the bottom of the hill they passed an old blue Volkswagen struggling gamely to negotiate the steep climb in the opposite direction.

'There's the police-station,' cried Simon, pointing across the main road as the car swept round the bend.

The car braked rapidly and turned right.

It was several seconds before the children realised that they were not on the road leading to the police-station, but in Clark's Lane, by which time Mr Barnes had braked to a halt, the doors were flung open and the Watchers dragged them from the car.

Seventeen

They were flung into the darkened room and as they sprawled to the ground they heard the heavy iron bolts drawn across the side of the door.

Sarah lay sobbing with shock, her hands and face scratched and bleeding. Simon, white with fear and anger pummelled his hands against the door. John slumped to the ground, his head spinning from a blow dealt by Bill Jeffs as he had struggled to free himself from the old man's clutches.

When the realisation of their plight had dawned on them they had fought like demons, but the Watchers were strong and had quickly overcome their attempts to break free. Simon had succeeded in weighing in with several vicious kicks before the sheer weight of numbers had borne him down.

'You bloody wait! Come back here, you sods!' Simon yelled through the door.

'It's no use.' John struggled to his feet. 'We're trapped. They've been prepared for this.' His voice was distant and resigned.

Sarah's sobs racked her body. The boys turned to comfort her.

'Calm down, Sarah. We'll sort it out, don't worry.' John wished with all his heart that he could believe his words. The game had been for grown-up stakes and they had just been children. Now it had caught up with them and they were going to have to pay the price.

Sarah's sobs died down.

'It's just too much!' she whispered through her tears.

'Mr Barnes, our own teacher! How could we ever have known? How on earth could he have been involved! What's going to happen now? We've got to get away! Get the police! Anybody!' Her voice rose hysterically.

John grabbed her arm.

'Stop it Sarah! Simon! Let's have a look at the room, there must be a window or something.'

They grasped the curtains and pulled.

Nothing happened.

Simon yanked harder. He was unable to find the seam.

John ducked his head under the material and came face to face with a row of heavy iron bars, freshly screwed into the woodwork. Beyond them the window panes had been painted over with white emulsion paint.

'We'll never get out this way!'

'What the hell are we going to do?' Panic crept back into Simon's voice.

'What's that?' John noticed a heavy object in the far corner of the room.

The first stone sat on its bed of velvet.

'It's your missing stone!' cried Simon.

They stared at it.

'A fat lot of good it did them too! I wish I'd never noticed that it had gone now!' said John bitterly.

Sarah was gradually coming to her senses.

'What happened?' she asked slowly.

'They grabbed us and threw us in here.'

'Is there any way out?'

'No, we've checked. Someone's gone to a lot of trouble to install bars across the windows. Like I said, we've been expected.'

'How long can they have known?'

The chill truth dawned on them.

'All the time. They've known all the time, right back to when we told Mr Barnes about the first stone. They've been watching us all along. Waiting, playing at cat and mouse, and then once we found out too much, bang! They sprung the trap.'

'What do you think they're going to do?' asked Simon fearfully.

'I don't know. How far will they go to keep their secret? Oh, I'm scared!' Sarah began to cry again.

Muffled voices filtered through the heavy door.

'Listen,' hissed John. 'Something's happening!'

The bolts rasped back and the door opened. Silhouetted against the harsh light of day the Watchers crowded in. No longer dressed in the clothes of the present day but in the dark vestments of mediaeval times. Cowls pulled low over their eyes. In the semi-darkness of the room their faces were hidden.

Sarah screamed.

Simon and John tensed themselves ready to fight.

Relentlessly they were edged back until the Watchers had forced them to the opposite wall.

The door closed and across the room a single candle flared into life. An old woman had entered clad in similar robes.

She stepped forward and the children looked into Mother Shipton's face.

'Welcome.'

Her voice was cold.

The Watchers bowed.

Simon broke the silence.

'I know you, you're the one who told us off about having our picnic up at the Stones! You'd best let us go now before we go to the police! When my Dad finds out about this, you'll be in a dead trouble!'

If she had smiled, or cursed Simon for a fool then it would have been a demonstration of her humanity. But she did neither. She continued as if their very existence was denied.

'The time is right.'

The Watchers heard the familiar words and a sigh passed from them. The children stood unable to move, frozen in fear and wonder at the dreadful scene.

Mother Shipton glided to the wall and silently the Watchers gathered about her. Her eyes blazed and Sarah felt as if her heart was about to burst. Her senses reeled and tears poured down her cheeks. The suffocating grasp that held her mind intensified and her reason began to slip away. With a groan she fell to the floor, unconscious.

'The Power is with us,' and now Mother Shipton smiled. From desperation and a terrible anger at Sarah's plight, John and Simon, without a word, leapt across the room and brought the old woman to the ground. The candle transcribed an arc and hurled molten wax across the robes of the nearest Watcher. Hardly had they reached the floor when strong and none too gentle hands pulled them from her and they were held fast, their hands pinned behind them.

'Pig-breed!' Bereft of dignity now, she spat upon the boys. 'See to them!'

She nodded to the first Watcher and the boys were dragged to the back of the room. A hand reached out and produced a roll of cellotape. Stripping off a layer the Watcher wrapped it tightly around John's mouth. Simon received the same treatment, and their hands were bound. Unceremoniously they were thrown to the floor.

Sarah moaned softly.

Mother Shipton adjusted her robes and pulled Sarah roughly to her side. She groaned again.

Mother Shipton held her firmly and with great precision dug her painted finger-nail into Sarah's ear-lobe. The girl yelped with pain.

'Listen.'

Sarah's eyes re-focused

The Watchers had gathered again beside the wall with Mother Shipton at the centre of the half-circle.

'You will watch, little one, and gaze your fill!'

Sarah tried to concentrate on her words but the awful seizure in her brain prevented her from grasping the significance of Mother Shipton's speech.

'So you have returned to us, little one! You seek again to spoil our Ways. Well, you may find your heart's desire. Watch now and see the forces I command, and for the short time that your life remains, know that nothing can destroy my power!'

Sarah tried to avert her eyes from Mother Shipton's gaze. She saw the Watchers, nearer now it seemed, their faces hidden, and strange words emerging from their throats, as Mother Shipton spoke.

The Words of Power rang out within the dusty room, but this time the first stone lay lifeless on its pedestal. What followed brought Sarah to the brink of madness.

The wall around which they stood was enveloped in a terrible flame. Cold and malignant, it picked out the contours of the stone. The Watchers stepped back as the flame intensified to a white glow and to Sarah's horror the central portion of the wall was revealed to be the Kingstone. Imprisoned between the wooden pillars of the room it writhed and faded in the hellish glare. This time the noise reached the threshold of physical pain, and three of the Watchers clapped their hands to their ears and screamed out their agony. Mother Shipton glanced at them with scarcely concealed contempt. Her eyes were upon Sarah, studying her closely. Sarah was suddenly aware how thin was the dividing line between their two minds. Almost as if at another time it could have been Sarah who stood there, arrogant in the usage of her power. The feeling of evil swept against her consciousness in waves. She dragged her eyes back to the wall.

The Kingstone was revealed in the sickly half-light, and as she watched it seemed to twist and bend, as if trying to gain release from the fires that burned within it.

Mother Shipton raised her head.

'I conjure you in the name of Her that first did touch your heart with stone!'

Throughout the room there echoed an eldritch wail, a cry of intense hatred. The thing that lay before them had suffered too long the tortures of its stony prison. To be reborn to face further torments was more than its raging soul could bear. The very fabric of the house seemed to melt around them as the giant forces now released wrestled with Mother Shipton's will.

As Sarah gazed up at the sheet of flame the features of the King began to form. Great hollow eyes stared in silence across the fiery curtain. The great body slumped forward with the weight of a thousand years.

Mother Shipton spoke again.

'I command you to tell the place from whence you travelled to your doom! The place of Appeasement!'

She stepped up to the malevolent image.

'Speak, before I return you to your timeless hell.'

The giant body quivered. It seemed to Sarah that for a moment its great eyes turned to look into hers and she was filled with the agonies that had been captured in its heart through all the centuries.

As her senses slid away from her, Sarah saw herself, robed in white, her hair long and buffeted by unseen winds. She saw again the dark brooding figures of her dreams. Suddenly her mind was touched by the tendrils of a power so strong that until that moment she could never have believed that it existed. Her thoughts were driven back to Long Compton Church and the figure in the doorway, and as the powers of True Wicca surged through her body, she became aware at last of who she really was, or who she had become.

As she gazed upon the manlike form that once had been a King she felt deep within her an answering chord of sympathy, as if in recognition of a fate that had once been her own.

Immediately the flame began to die.

The face dissolved until at last the eyes alone remained.

Almost a look of gratitude mirrored in the pockets of empty stone.

Mother Shipton went berserk. Leaping to the wall she clawed and hammered with her hands.

'Return! Return! I conjure you! By the powers that I command. Return!'

The flame died.

Sarah stood erect.

Against the wall Mother Shipton scrabbled and cursed. The Watchers glanced at one another, unsure as to what had happened, unsure as to what to do.

'The Power has gone!' Mother Shipton screamed in rage. A madwoman. All reason fled.

Suddenly she turned from the wall. The Watchers stood, anonymous, afraid of what was to come.

Her hand came up and pointed waveringly at the girl.

'This is your doing! You return to destroy my Power!' She leapt at Sarah.

Sarah flinched, expecting to be struck to the ground.

Mother Shipton's voice was a terrible whisper.

'I shall repay you for this, my little one!'

She edged towards her, her fingers working.

'Wait Mother!'

She spun around to confront the voice. It was Mr Barnes.

'You dare to intercede?'

'No! Oh, no, Mother!'

She pushed him to one side and returned her attention to Sarah.

She raised her arms and Sarah closed her eyes.

'We have dealt with you before. By the Power that remains within me, return to your slumber! And seek never to deny the Shiptons again!'

That was all.

A deadly weariness began to creep over Sarah's body.

What had happened? What had Mother Shipton said?

'Listen Mother.' It was Mr Barnes again.

'What maunderings now?'

'I feel she knows more than we thought. She has the Power. Even I can see that. I've seen what she has done to you here tonight. I reckon she knows a lot more than we think about our search.'

Sarah fought the sleepiness that was struggling to lay hold of her.

Mother Shipton placed her cracked and splitting lips against Sarah's ear.

'Is this true, my little one?'

From another universe she heard Mother Shipton's voice but she could find no strength to reply.

'Brat! Are you so unconcerned with your fate that you can afford to feign indifference? Your friends must know of the stone effigy that lies upon the steps of Long Compton Church. But do they know, as you do, how first she came to lie there? She came to threaten our Power and now she rots in stone. Need I say more?'

Sarah stood silent.

Not so Simon. From his place on the floor he began to writhe and moan through his gag.

Mother Shipton did not fail to notice this.

'I think our little fighting cock wishes to add a word!'

The Watchers stepped forward and the cellotape was cruelly wrenched from Simon's lips. He spoke through blood that now tricked down his chin.

'For God's sake tell 'em, Sarah. She'll kill yer if yer don't!'

Mother Shipton lowered her face to a level with Simon. She had hoped that one of the boys would break. She had had no such illusion about the girl. The Power she now possessed would give her courage to remain silent whatever the threat.

'Tell me then,' she whispered encouragingly.

'I only know about the marking,' Simon stopped and looked up in anguish as Sarah cursed him for a fool.

'A marking?' Mother Shipton's eyes gleamed. 'Speak it and the girl goes free,' she wheedled.

John lay helpless to prevent him speaking. Sarah cursed and screamed as if her voice would drown the secrets that Simon spoke.

'I dunno what it is, we couldn't work it out!' he stammered.

Mother Shipton thrust her face into his.

'The girl's life depends on it,' she snarled.

'It's …. it's on a piece of paper … in John's pocket.'

Simon stuttered the words in terror. Mother Shipton pushed him to the floor.

'Get it,' she spat the order to the Watchers.

They grasped John and within seconds the scrap of paper was in her hand.

She gazed at the cipher.

'This is a remnant of a Carolingian script.'

Her eyes ran quickly over the markings.

'I must consult the writings in our family's book, for this is a place-name in the elder tongue.'

Her voice cracked into laughter.

'So the answer was there all the time!'

Simon squirmed.

'Let her go! You said you'd let her go!'

'Farewell child!' she almost smiled as she gathered up her robes. 'You have spoken truly and helped us much. I shall not forget your reward. Your faithfulness is touching. Be rewarded, your end shall be the same as hers. Mark well the reason for the olden tale that Rollright Stones cannot be counted! How do you think the legend came about? What better burial place for those who in the past have sought my family's power. And for their marking place, another stone! The perfect hiding place, for amongst so many, who would note an extra one? Know now that in a few short hours my Words will have brought your interference to an end and we shall add three more headstones to the Rollright Circle!'

She swept out of the room, laughing, and the Watchers silently followed.

Mother Shipton almost ran to collect the ancient book. Quickly she leafed through its pages. 'CUMBROC. CUMBROC. I know the place! Our plans have not yet gone astray. All that remains is for us to travel there and gain the treasure. Prepare yourselves. Our time of triumph is come!'

Bill Jeffs grasped her sleeve.

'The children, what of them?'

'They shall be buried on our return. Get Barnes to see that they are properly secured, particularly the girl. We must take no risk of their escape before the Words have taken their effect.'

Bill Jeffs hurried off to find Mr Barnes and some more rope. Hastily Sarah was bound and gagged, and fresh bands of cellotape were wrapped around Simon's mouth. He struggled furiously, the knowledge of his betrayal stinging his senses. Without further ado the children were flung against the far wall, their breath knocked from their bodies.

Mr Barnes and Bill Jeffs hurried from the room giving the children a last cursory glance. The door slammed and the bolts were drawn.

The children heard the sound of a heavy starter-motor being engaged. The engine fired and revved up. The sounds inside the house died away, a final door banged shut and silence descended. They heard the vehicle accelerate away down the Lane and onto the main road.

Sarah lay huddled against the wall. The strange sleepiness that had enveloped her had worn off for a moment. Beside her lay the two boys. She tried to twist her head in order to free her mouth of cellotape. If she could only manage to do that there might be a chance of biting though it. But it had been applied in such quantity that it was impossible to curl her lip around it.

John squirmed on the floor. He felt a weariness in his arms and legs and could move only with great effort.

Simon was numb. His joints ached as if he had a heavy cold. The Power was slowly and insidiously carrying out its work.

Simon and John stared hard at one another. Simon tried to blink his eyes at John but the effort was too much for him. He was unable to signal the correct muscles.

'We've got to do something soon,' thought John, 'otherwise it'll be too late for any of us.'

As if by telepathy Sarah suddenly jerked herself against the wall and fell onto her side. She struggled upright and tried to manoeuvre her head against a jutting piece of stonework. Her idea was to rub the cellotape against the edge and rip it. Then at least she could communicate with the boys. She began to move her cheek frantically against the stone. The pain was dreadful. The effort of will that it took to force herself to willingly scrape away the skin on her face was too much and she slipped to the ground sobbing.

Gradually, she became aware of a change in the surface of the stone. A soft glow appeared. She thought she must be passing out again. Her head slumped onto the stonework. The glow seemed to focus on her. By now both John and Simon could see it, and summoning all their strength they tried to lever themselves into an upright position.

Sarah seemed unconscious.

In her mind she heard a voice, and out of the darkness that filled her thoughts came the girl with her face. She saw her more clearly than ever before. It was *her* face, but a Sarah of a few years from now. Still beautiful, but lined with cares that she as yet did not know. Her voice was gentle and reassuring. Sarah knew that this girl was the Last True Witch of Rollright and that she had joined Sarah's spirit in one final effort to rid the world of the evil of Shipton's brood. In those few moments of unconsciousness she renewed in Sarah the power of Wicca and left in her mind the knowledge of goodness and peace.

A crackling sound filled the air and Simon and John watched as the cellotape covering Sarah's mouth began to blacken and melt, as if in a fierce flame. Yet Sarah's skin remained untouched. She groaned and raised her head. Her face streamed with blood from the grazes she had inflicted on herself.

'I don't understand.'

She opened her eyes. There was the Kingstone. Within its heart the flame burned. Tentatively she raised her hands behind her back and touched the surface of the stone. A smell of charring hemp filled the room. Within seconds the bonds that had held her fell in blackened strands to the floor.

'Simon, John, quickly!' She hobbled towards them and hauled them against the stone. As the cold flame ate through their cords she pulled the cellotape from their lips. They tried to rise, but fell again, forgetting the bindings on their legs. The numbness and aching had fled from their limbs with the touch of the flame. They attacked the ropes that still held them, and only when this was done did they turn to one another and embrace, their bodies trembling with the ordeal. Tears ran down their faces and uncaring, Simon hugged Sarah and John until his strength gave out.

'I'm sorry. I'm sorry I let yer down,' he wept.

John ruffled his hair,' and Sarah tried to smile, but tears kept reforming in her eyes.

'It doesn't matter. It doesn't matter now,' she whispered.

'We've just got to get out of here and get some help.'

John was already regaining some of his composure.

'You seemed to have had some already,' he said quietly.

They turned to look at the Kingstone. It stood mute and immovable as it had done for centuries up on the hillside, and of the flame there was no sign.

'What about her curse?' gasped John. 'How do you feel, Simon?'

Simon was rubbing his arms and legs. 'I'll feel all right I reckon once I've got my circulation back.'

He tried to grin. 'It's just me arms and legs still feel a bit stiff!'

John nodded in agreement. 'Mine too, but that's with being tied up for so long. I don't think she can harm us, do you?'

'I think she's just having us on,' replied Simon. 'I reckon Sarah has done something to her magic. It don't seem to work properly when she's around.'

'I hope you're right,' said Sarah. It was true. The boys did look better. But Sarah well knew there was no doubt as to the ability of Mother Shipton to kill them all. The question was, would her new power serve to protect them until Mother Shipton could be brought to book?

'Let's get out of here for God's sake!' Simon was searching the room for some means of escape.

'We've checked the window, that's no good,' said John.

'That leaves the door. But how do you get through solid wood, with iron bolts on the other side?'

'I saw a film once,' Simon reminisced. 'It was where these baddies were trying to get into a castle. It had a great big door so they got a batterin' ram and knocked it down.'

'We're a bit short of battering rams unfortunately,' retorted John. 'Wait a minute though. Remember what's over there! He pointed to the far side of the room where the first missing stone still lay.

'It might just do at that!' cried Sarah.

They tried to lift it. It was incredibly heavy. Their faces contorted with effort as they raised it from the table and edged it towards the door.

'Right,' announced John. 'We'll take it a few steps back and charge the door with it.'

They dropped the stone to the floor and rested their arms for a moment.

'Mother Shipton must have known what our marking meant,' said John, rubbing his aching wrists.

'Yes,' said Sarah. 'That's where they've gone. To get the treasure.'

'So what do we do when we get out?' asked John. 'Go to the police?'

'There's no time.'

'How do you mean?'

'By the time we explain the story to the police, Mother Shipton will have found the treasure, discovered we've escaped, and she and the Watchers will disappear with the loot!'

'So what then?'

'If we get out of here our best bet is Dave Coulbeck. He'll help.'

'How?'

'Maybe we could catch them up. They can't have got far, they must be in a large vehicle. I heard them start it.'

'That's plain ridiculous, if you don't mind me saying so,' said John. 'How many different side roads and lanes do you know within a quarter of a mile of here? They could have taken any one of them. You'd never find them!'

'It'd be best to go to the police,' said Simon decisively.

'Let's just get out of here first,' said Sarah in a heartfelt voice. 'Come on Samson!'

'Heave!'

The three children strained and lifted the stone to waist height. Staggering as fast as they could they gained momentum and the massive weight struck the door. They heard the bolts shudder on the other side.

'Watch out!'

The stone slipped from their hands and bounced onto the ground.

'Again!'

They hauled the stone back and charged.

This time there was the sound of protesting metal and the door yielded an inch.

'This time should do it!' gasped Simon.

They hurled themselves at the door and with a splintering crash the bolts snapped and it yawned open. The stone crashed to the floor, its work done.

'That's it!' yelled John. 'Let's get out of here!'

They scrambled through the rooms that led to the front of the house, opened the door that led to the outside and without turning back they fled up the lane towards Dave Coulbeck's house.

Eighteen

The hammering on the door roused Dave Coulbeck from a deep sleep. At first he thought the baby had woken and was crying.

His wife turned towards him.

'Your turn for the feed love,' she murmured, and fell back into her dream.

Dave focused his mind on the source of the noise. Silently he slipped out of bed, and pulling on his dressing gown he made his way downstairs. As he flicked on the hall light he glanced at his watch. Half-past four. It was nearly morning. Who on earth could it be at this hour? The police? Had there been an accident or something? He fumbled with the door catch. The hammering increased with intensity.

'Who is it?' he called as he lifted the safety-chain. 'What do you want?'

'Oh please, please open the door!' Sarah's voice was cracked with tension.

The youngsters! What the hell were they doing here at this time of the morning?

He flung open the door and the three children stumbled inside. Dave's shocked gaze bore witness to the cuts and bruises they had received.

'What the Devil's been happening to you?' he exclaimed.

'It's a long story!' gasped John. 'We need your help. Our theories about Mother Shipton and her friends were true. We were led into a trap up at the Rollrights. You'd never believe it but one of her helpers has turned out to be our teacher, Mr Barnes!'

Dave stared at them in astonishment.

'You'd best tell me all about it! This has turned into a very serious matter. I think we'd best call the police and then I'll get something for your cuts.'

He headed towards the telephone in the hallway.

'No! No, you mustn't do that!' cried Sarah. 'There's no time! They know where the treasure is, Simon told them about the marking and they

106

got the paper with it on from John, and she recognised it. They drove off as soon as they could after that.'

'She's not the only one to know where it is,' interrupted Dave.

It was the children's turn to look astonished.

'You mean you worked out the code?'

'Well, not exactly.'

He told them briefly of his visit to the County Records Office and the name that had been engraved on the Kingstone.

'So where is Cumbroc?' The children were on tenterhooks.

'Its name hasn't changed much,' said Dave. 'It's now called Combrook and it's somewhere between the villages of Kineton and Wellesbourne. I'd never heard of it before.'

'How do you know it's the right place?' queried John.

'Everything fits together,' explained Dave. 'The fragment of lettering from your clue spells out "Cumbroc" and that was the name of the place at least eight hundred years ago. Also there's a lake!'

'We'd best get a move on,' ordered Sarah. 'That's where they'll be, trying to lay their hands on the treasure. We've got to get there and stop them!'

'I still say that is a job for the police now,' counselled Dave. 'There's nothing you can do on your own. Just take a look at yourselves. You're absolutely exhausted!'

He refrained from adding that they were also children and that these people were obviously extremely dangerous.

'No!' said Sarah. 'I've got to get there. Her powers have to be broken, and only I can stop her.'

She rapidly told of the events that occurred in Mother Shipton's cottage. How she had been invested with a power that had caused the re-birth of the Kingstone to come to an end, and how the flame had appeared, to help them in their escape.

'If we go to the police, Mother Shipton and her helpers will just lie low, together with the treasure, and her powers will still remain.'

'I don't seem to have any choice in the matter,' said Dave slowly. He sensed the new dominance of Sarah's personality. 'Just give me time to get dressed and to tell the wife that I'm going out. Though heaven knows how I'm going to explain all this to her!'

He paused as he realised how tired the children must be, and the fresh dangers they were going to face.

'Sarah, go and put a pan on the stove and heat up a couple of tins of soup. I daresay you could do with it. It'll warm us up before we go.'

Sarah hunted out a pan and some tins and switched on the electric cooker.

Simon and John were so tired that their eyelids began to close almost as soon as they had finished their soup. Sarah however was wide awake. Dave had gone upstairs to explain to his wife, and she could hear a muffled conversation being held up in the bedroom.

Suddenly she recalled Mother Shipton's curse.

'Hey! Simon, John! Do you still feel OK?'

'Yes,' replied John. 'Just very, very sleepy.'

'Me too!' added Simon, and yawned to lend weight to his words.

Sarah cast a worried glance at them both. She was extremely concerned about the effect of Mother Shipton's words on the two boys. She had no way of knowing how far her own powers could counteract the witch's curse. She didn't really want to risk them going to Combook. Yet their condition made it more urgent than ever. She hoped whatever confrontation occurred, that somehow she could overcome Mother Shipton and free them from the spell, otherwise it would be the end for all of them.

Dave Coulbeck appeared in the doorway wearing a heavy tartan lumber-jacket. He pulled on a pair of driving gloves as he spoke.

'We'd best be off!'

'Oh, thanks, thanks for everything!' cried Sarah, and flung her arms around him. 'You don't realise how important this is!'

'Perhaps I do,' replied Dave softly. 'Perhaps I do!'

They stepped out of the front door and into the biting cold of the early morning. The children stamped their feet as Dave started the Volkswagen and backed it into the Lane. 'Jump in!'

The car swirled exhaust fumes into the frozen air as they drove through the sleeping village. The night was still dark and the stars burned coldly above Long Compton. The road was clear of traffic at that time of the morning.

Sarah wiped her frosted breath from the inside of the windscreen as Dave sped into the countryside.

Simon and John lay dozing in the back seat. Sarah snatched an occasional glance at them. Was it just weariness or something more sinister?

Simon snored loudly and jerked awake.

The car rattled into Shipston-on-Stour and weaved through the narrow streets. A solitary workman cycled from a house into the road. Dave flashed his lights in warning and pulled past.

What were they going to do when they arrived at Combrook? Dave pondered the question as he drove. He realised that something very strange had happened back in Clark's Lane, and that Sarah was no longer quite the same person. Basic and long-forgotten powers were involved. Elemental powers, shared by both Mother Shipton and Sarah. Whatever the outcome he felt a terrible responsibility for the safety of the children, yet he was helpless. He had felt the strength of Sarah's will back at his house, when she had persuaded him to take them to Combrook. But was it strong enough to combat this evil woman and her helpmates? He doubted it. Secretly he resolved that should Mother Shipton gain the upper hand he would telephone the police whether Sarah agreed or not. After all, they were only children!

Sarah herself had no real idea as to what course of action she should take. She simply knew that within her lay the power to stop Mother Shipton. At all costs she must be prevented from obtaining the treasure. Sarah pledged herself to preserve its rightful resting place.

They travelled into the first grey light of dawn. Onto the Fosse Way and along a straight road tunnelling through the darkness. At last a signpost blinked into life in the car headlights.

'Combrook.'

'There it is!' shrieked Sarah. John and Simon were instantly awake.

Dave hurled the car across the main road and they scuttled down a narrow lane with trees on their left and open fields to their right. The road fell away rapidly and the car involuntarily increased its speed. It bounced between two gate posts and they whirled past the place-name sign. A sharp corner loomed ahead and they dropped into the hidden village.

Combrook lay in its blanket of wood smoke. A neat collection of thatched cottages interspersed with new houses. It mirrored a hundred other small half-forgotten villages in the county. No street lights obscured the moonlight. Frosted clouds chased across the sky and the pale silvery light waxed and waned. People who lived there said they put the lid on Combrook at night.

As the car sped into the village the children scoured the landscape for a glimpse of the lake.

Nothing.

The car hurtled around a hair-pin bend and began to pull uphill. Ahead the road forked. The main part appeared to rise beyond the church and disappear at the top of the hill. Dave swerved right to follow it and the engine laboured as the car began to climb. There was still no lake in sight.

Dave reached the crest of the hill and pulled the car into the side of the road. He opened the door and crunched into the icy verge. Already the light was beginning to strengthen across the fields and the darkness was no longer absolute.

Sarah clambered out after him. John and Simon lay huddled together in the back of the car, still feeling dazed and sleepy.

'Look! Over there!' Sarah was pointing across the fields towards a thick wood. 'I'm sure I saw the glint of water just beyond that first clump of trees.'

Dave strained his eyes. Was it water reflected in the moonlight?

'That must be it! We never saw it on our way into the village!' exclaimed Sarah. 'Let's go on a little further.'

They climbed back into the car and Dave raced the engine. Sarah's cheeks tingled with the cold. They drove on, but soon realised that they were heading away from the place where Sarah had seen the reflection.

'Stop here!' shouted Sarah suddenly, and such was the power in her voice, that Dave instinctively obeyed.

'There's a farm gate with PRIVATE on it.' She pointed through the back window at the gate-way that was illuminated in the red glare of the Volkswagen's brake lights.

'It looks as if it leads in the right direction. In for a penny, in for a pound,' muttered Dave, and reversed the car along the road until the gate-way lay ahead of them again. Sarah opened the car door.

'I'll open the gate!' She lifted the catch and swung it open. The car bounced forward onto a rut filled-filled track.

'This'll do my suspension no good, MOT or no MOT!' said Dave cheerily as Sarah rejoined him. The boys had woken and were beginning to take an interest in the proceedings once again. The car clattered down the track. Suddenly the path ahead veered sharply to the right. Dave pulled hard on the wheel but the car was slow to respond and it slid inelegantly from the pathway and the front wing collided with a tree. The lights dimmed. Dave cursed loudly and rammed it into reverse.

The wheels spun and turned the frozen mud to liquid. The car sank into the mire. Embedded in the tree and unable to break free of the mud it was well and truly stuck.

'What do we do now?' groaned John.

Before anyone could stop her Sarah leapt out of the car and vanished down the track beyond the range of the headlights.

Dave jumped out after her.

'Hey! You daft thing! Come back!' His voice was absorbed totally by the dense woodland. She had gone.

He turned to John and Simon who were struggling out of the car and onto the track.

'You'd best get after her! Stop here! I'll try and get the car back on the path and follow you. Keep to the track so that I won't lose you. Here!' He threw John his torch. 'For God's sake find her before she does something stupid!'

John and Simon ran on as best they could, but their legs felt heavy as lead, and their heads were spinning as they raced over the rock-hard ground, trying their best to avoid the fallen branches and other debris that was picked up in the wavering beam of the torch.

'I thought I saw her then!' gasped Simon. 'Straight ahead!'

They scrambled over a fallen tree-trunk that spanned the path-way.

John clattered to a halt.

'That's torn it!'

'Eh?' spluttered Simon.

'That tree! Dave'll never get his car beyond that!'

'One of us had better go back and warn him.'

'Go on then, get back. Tell him I've gone ahead. If this leads to the lake I'll meet you both there!'

Simon leapt over the trunk and hurried back along the track.

John halted for a moment.

He listened.

He could hear Simon's footsteps pounding into the distance.

Ahead everything was as silent as the grave. Cautiously, aware that he was now completely alone, he edged forward.

Nineteen

The Watchers had hurriedly climbed into the powerful Land Rover that was parked outside Mother Shipton's cottage. She was already seated next to Mr Barnes in the front seat.

He gunned the engine and as the last of the Watchers flung picks, shovels and themselves into the back, he eased his foot off the clutch and accelerated down the lane.

The journey to Combrook passed in silence. Each was busy with his own thoughts. Mother Shipton sat calm and composed watching the road unwind ahead.

As the Land Rover roared down the hillside into the village of Combrook, Mr Barnes glanced across at Mother Shipton.

'If this treasure is at the bottom of the lake, how do we get it?' he asked. 'I know you've had this truck all prepared for many months now, but I would have thought we would have needed diving equipment and special apparatus. What good are picks and shovels if it lies 50 feet below water?'

The Watchers muttered their agreement.

Mother Shipton folded her arms.

'Do you still have so little faith in my powers?' she asked icily. 'After all that has passed this night do you still doubt my power over the elements of earth, air, fire and water?'

Silence fell again. She nodded briefly and the Land Rover veered left past the church and into a narrow lane that led to the lake.

At the end of the lane lay a private roadway leading to an old game-keeper's cottage. The public right of way ended a short way before this point, where a row of converted thatched cottages stood.

Mr Barnes pulled the Land Rover into the side, and switching on his torch he consulted a detailed Ordnance Survey map of the area.

'We can get to the lake along this old pathway,' he indicated with his finger. 'We can get the Land Rover as far as here.' His finger stabbed the map again. 'But from that point we shall have to travel on foot.'

He extinguished the light and the Land Rover plunged down the track. Soon they came to the footpath.

'This is as far as we go.'

The Watchers climbed stiffly down from the truck and began to collect the equipment from the back. Heavy duty torches, picks, shovels and numerous coils of rope.

Silently they formed a column and led by Mother Shipton they began to climb the bank that led to the lake side.

The ground was marshy and treacherous underfoot and their shoes sank obscenely into the black mud.

Sarah ran headlong, unaware of the tree trunk that blocked the path. It caught her legs and she fell heavily. Her head cracked against the ground. She staggered to her feet and blinked away the tears. She ran on until the path began to widen. Ahead lay the lake, cold and deep, a winter sky etched on its surface. The wind rippled occasionally across the reflection and Sarah glanced upwards half expecting to see the ripples mirrored in the sky.

She stood at the lake side. Her ears picked up a soft whispering. She turned her head in its direction. An abrasive distant sound. Hypnotic and continuous.

She returned her gaze to the water. There was no sign of Mother Shipton and her friends. Had Dave been right? Perhaps this wasn't the place after all.

Suddenly her doubts vanished. Across the curve of the lake something was happening that did not belong to the safe ordinary world she had inhabited until tonight.

Mother Shipton stood at the water's edge. The Watchers threw down their tools and gathered around her. A roaring broke the silence. She lifted her arms to enfold the lake.

The Words of Power echoed across the waters.

The cold bit into their faces as they watched.

Mother Shipton waited, her arms still outstretched.

Slowly, about a hundred yards from the shore the lake began to move. It broke into ripples. The Watchers lifted their heads to observe the change.

Steadily the ripples curved back upon themselves and a vortex formed. Faster now the waters spun, and with the increase in speed they lifted from the surface of the lake to form a column 30 feet high. There was something terribly life-like about its movement, as if it possessed an intelligence of its own. It swayed and rolled, black against the changing sky.

Gradually it began to move. It snaked across the surface first one way and then another. Almost as if it were scenting its prey. Deliberately, so it seemed, it sped across the lake, homing in on some long forgotten pulse.

Their eyes watched it travel, until it became one with the sound that had been with them since their arrival.

'Come!' cried Mother Shipton, and they followed obediently at her heels as she swept towards the fence that barred the way to where the column whirled suspended, a short distance from the shore.

As they hurried after her they became aware of the increasing volume of noise. They rushed along the lakeside path and stopped in amazement as Mother Shipton came face to face with the column. It hovered blackly over the source of the thunderous roar.

An ancient slip sump, built countless years ago to help the drainage of the lake. A deep shaft of hand-hewn stone over which plunged the waters to find their way to the brook that meandered 50 feet below.

'The fools have built this water-shaft upon the place of Appeasement!' Mother Shipton exclaimed. 'But their mindless tampering has helped us. We need have no worries about obtaining our reward. This pit can be reached from under the hillside. We must retrace our footsteps and find the tunnel that leads back to this place. A drenching will be a small price to pay for what we'll find beneath!'

The Watchers glanced at one another, traces of excitement showing in their faces. Mr Barnes was the first one to move. He hurried back to where the tools were lying, and grasping a pick he hurled himself down the hillside towards the sound of fast flowing water. Throwing all caution to the wind, the Watchers ran after him, afraid he might find the treasure first. Mother Shipton peered up at the towering column of water.

'So my powers have not yet been diminished,' she gloated, and slowly picked her way down the embankment in the direction in which the Watchers had gone.

Sarah watched the water-spout. It could only be the work of Mother Shipton. But what was it? It seemed to her that it possessed a mind of its own, circling the lake for what seemed an age, and then, as if it had come to some important decision, it began to move steadily towards a point near the shore about half a mile away. Without really knowing why, Sarah began to stumble along the path that skirted the lakeside, heading towards the distant spout.

The track was strewn with fallen branches and half hidden stones but she staggered on, keeping one eye always on the swirling water that rose above the lake.

The roaring became louder.

Simon saw the headlights of the car ahead.

'Hang on! Wait a minute!' he shouted.

Dave's head peered out of the window.

'Simon! What are you doing back here?'

Simon hurriedly told him about the fallen tree, and how John had gone on ahead.

'Any sign of Sarah?' asked Dave anxiously.

'I dunno,' replied Simon. 'I thought I caught sight of her in the distance but it was hard to tell in this light.'

'Perhaps John will have found her by now,' said Dave hopefully. 'It's a good job you came back in a way, I can't budge this car. Perhaps if you give me a hand ...'

Simon's legs were getting even weaker and his fingers were becoming stiff.

'All right, let's 'ave a go!'

Dave showed him how to rev the engine and engage the clutch.

'I'll try and lever this branch under the wheel,' he explained.

'Tell us when yer ready!'

Dave shoved the branch into the mud and jammed it against the tyre.

'Now!'

The engine roared and Dave forced the branch harder against the wheel. Simon lifted the clutch and the wheels spun against the new obstruction. Mud spattered against Dave's coat. The rear wheels wobbled crazily in the rut and suddenly the tyre gripped and the car was flung backwards.

'Help!' yelled Simon, as he desperately tried to control the car. He lifted his foot from the clutch and the engine struggled and died. The car rolled forward again into the rut.

'Bloody hell!' he jumped from the driver's seat, his face white.

'Come on, jump in,' shouted Dave, squirming into the driving position. 'Let me have another try!'

Simon stood against the passenger door, his fingers would no longer do what he wanted.

'I can't,' he said stupidly.

Dave opened the door using the inside catch.

'What's the matter?'

Simon was crying.

'It's me hands! They don't work no more!' he sobbed, and Dave noticed that his speech was slurred.

Before he could reach out his hand to help him inside, Simon's eyes closed and he crumpled to the ground.

Dave ran to the other side of the car and gently lifted him into the back seat. Simon showed no sign of movement and his breathing was laboured.

'Shock!' muttered Dave, and reached into the luggage space for a travelling rug. He wrapped it around Simon and made sure he was as comfortable as possible.

'This game's gone on long enough,' he decided. 'I've lost two of them, and the third one's lying here half dead. It's time I got hold of the police!'

He locked the doors of the car and strode off back up the track.

Mr Barnes, followed closely by the remaining Watchers, scrambled down the hillside and into the stream that flowed towards the village. The water was icy cold and their shoes were soon waterlogged. Clutching their picks and shovels, and with heavy coils of rope wrapped around their waists, they struggled upwards to the head of the brook, until they came to a long dank tunnel that ended at the base of the sump.

A cascade of freezing water rebounded onto the stone floor of the shaft. Mr Barnes reached the opening and a deluge of water engulfed him, knocking the breath from his body and drenching him to the bone in an instant.

Oblivious to the chill he slithered across the slippery, moss covered stones and steadied himself against the walls of the shaft. He raised his pick and began to smash into the slabs that lined the bottom of the pit.

Within moments the other Watchers had joined him and soon the entire floor had been torn up, loose earth and small chips of stone instantly flushed away by the relentless torrent.

Blinking and cursing, the continual downpour beating at their heads and shoulders, they hacked and clawed deeper into the base.

Mother Shipton picked her way delicately over a series of stepping stones which lead with precision to the head of the tunnel. She stood silently observing the efforts of the Watchers and allowed herself only the flicker of a smile when Bill Jeff's pick rang against metal.

Sarah had lost all track of time. How long it had taken her to travel from where she had first seen the water spout she had no idea. Although only a bare half mile as the crow flies, her journey had involved countless obstacles which in the half-light had caused her to trip and fall. A weariness invaded her mind as well as her body and she had to force herself not to succumb to the wonderful idea of curling up on the frost covered pathway and falling asleep.

A roaring noise echoed in her ears. She listened more carefully. That sound. Was it the column of water? She peered through the line of bushes that dipped into the lake. Just ahead the towering mass of the column whirled and eddied above a circular pit into which disappeared the surplus waters of the lake. The thunder of the falling water began to exert an hypnotic effect on her.

A waterfall and a waterspout. What did it mean? The answer obviously lay within the depths of the shaft. Without a thought as to the danger involved Sarah reached the edge of the lake and stepped in. The water instantly chilled her feet and pain rocketed through her body. She waded out towards the gaping blackness of the pit. As she forced her legs to carry her nearer she suddenly heard voices, muttered and indistinct, coming from the shaft. Spurred on, she reached the edge, her feet sliding and shifting on the oily surface of the pebbles that lined the lake bottom. The downward motion of the water caught her eye and her balance was swept away. She regained her footing and inched her way to the lip of the sump. She peered over the edge. Above her the water spout spun and swayed silently. For one fleeting moment she imagined that she caught sight of a shadowy figure moving through the deluge that thundered onto the floor of the shaft. She blinked her eyes and it was gone.

At that moment a dreadful premonition filled her, and she glanced upwards at the water spout. Its whirling centre slowed and then stopped. Instantly it collapsed inwards, crushing her with a terrible weight of freezing water. The blow hit her on the shoulders and she was knocked forward into the shaft.

She saw the black mouth gape open to receive her, and felt her body sprawl towards it. Suddenly she was hurled backwards to land with a splash in the shallows, several feet from the mouth of the sump. Her head disappeared briefly beneath the surface and she emerged coughing and retching up the foul liquid she had swallowed. She saw John, up to his knees in water, leaning over her.

'John!' she cried, and clambered against his legs until she was upright once more. 'But how did you know where I was?'

John grasped her hand and dragged her towards the shore.

'Let's get out of this water before we die of exposure,' he gasped, his teeth rattling relentlessly.

He pulled himself on to the bank and hauled Sarah up after him.

'It wasn't too difficult to find you,' he spluttered. 'I got to the lakeside and saw that pillar of water. I guessed you'd probably be heading for it, and I was right. I got here just as you were paddling out to the waterfall. I didn't shout in case you missed your footing, but when I saw you get so close to the edge I was terrified that you'd fall, so I waded in after you. It's a good job I did. If I hadn't grabbed you that fall of water would have knocked you right over the edge.'

'I think that's what it was intended to do,' declared Sarah.

'Either that, or it had served its purpose and they've found the treasure. I'm sorry I left you and Dave and Simon.'

She tried to squeeze some of the water from her anorak.

'I just had to go on. I had to try and find her,' her voice broke. 'I didn't manage it though, did I?'

She remembered the figure in the shaft.

'But they can't be far away. I'm sure I saw something at the bottom of the waterfall. I heard voices, that's why I leaned over!'

John stood silent.

Sarah glanced across to the wood.

'I reckon they've found another way out. Look! The ground slopes away just ahead, down towards the village. I bet if we head that way we'll meet up with them! Perhaps I can stop them!'

John made no reply.

'What on earth's the matter? You look as if you've seen a ghost!'

John's teeth were clenched together and he was shivering violently.

'I can't move,' he grated. His eyes were staring, wide with fear. Sarah didn't hesitate. She threw her arms around his shoulders and half lifted, half dragged him down the path that fell away to the village.

Twenty

The Watchers emerged from the tunnel, half-drowned but victorious, bearing their picks, shovels and ropes in a triumphal procession. Bill Jeffs, Mr Barnes, and two others splashed through the stream hauling a cumbersome load. Mother Shipton watched in silent approval as they filed past her and continued down the brook towards the pathway. They clambered onto dry land, and barely pausing to regain their breath, hurried through the gate and up to the parked Land Rover.

The early morning light began to pick out the colours of the wood from the surrounding greyness. Tendrils of mist curled upward from the surface of the lake and wafted like lost souls down the hillside.

It was still too early for any villagers to be about. If there had been any they would have been extremely curious to know what pursuit required a group of grown men led by a rather elderly lady to be wandering around drenched to the skin.

Carefully, they dragged their load onto the tailgate of the Land Rover and lifted it inside. Mr Barnes hastily covered it with sacks, and the tools were thrown on top to add extra camouflage. The Watchers squelched aboard and Mother Shipton and Mr Barnes heaved themselves into the front seats, steam rising from their clothing as they began to warm up.

Mr Barnes pressed the starter and the engine burst into life. The lane end was narrow and it took several turns, each accompanied by a thunderous clashing of gears before the Land Rover was able to make its way back onto the main road.

The Land Rover gathered speed and swerved past the church and up the hill that led out of the village.

'My powers have not failed us!' exulted Mother Shipton. 'The Treasure of Appeasement is ours! The greatest deed of the Shiptons is complete. My line will not die in vain! For over a thousand years that treasure has rightfully belonged to us and now I have it!'

'There's just one thing,' reminded Mr Barnes. 'Those children, we've got to deal with them when we get back.'

'Have no worries on that score,' crowed Mother Shipton confidently. 'When we return they will be dead and we can take them to the Circle. They will never be heard of again. The last time they were seen was at the Rollrights. If the police make their inquiries they will begin and end there.'

The Watchers smiled to themselves.

Sarah had succeeded in reaching the gateway to the lane where Mother Shipton and the Watchers had parked. However she had been unable to catch up with them. John had become all but unconscious, and was no longer capable of walking or even supporting himself. His limbs were stiff and awkward and it had taken every scrap of strength that Sarah possessed to stumble with him to the gate.

As they approached the gateway Sarah heard the sound of an engine being started and realised that they were too late. Mother Shipton was making good her escape.

With this realisation the cold, shock and terror of the night swept over her and she fell to the ground with John sprawled on top of her.

She found herself high upon a hillside. She was clothed in white and her long hair hung low over her shoulders. The sky was starless and a cold searching wind blew around her.

She had waited for so long.

She looked down the hill.

At last they were coming.

And now she knew what it was she had to do.

Mr Barnes saw the girl standing in the roadway. She lifted her arms in greeting as Mother Shipton's eyes met hers. With a cry of recognition Mr Barnes swung the wheel of the Land Rover to the left and his final vision was of the girl, her arms still outstretched, and behind her a wall of dark and threatening figures. In her eyes was a look of sublime revenge.

The Land Rover swerved across the road in a last desperate effort to escape, when its body was crushed under a ghastly and incalculable weight. With a scream of rending metal the whole vehicle folded together, unbelievable stresses fracturing every seam of its skeleton. With a blast that wakened every house in the village, the petrol tank exploded and the wreckage was engulfed in flames.

Dave Coulbeck had almost reached the end of the track when he was stopped dead by a violent crash followed almost immediately by a loud explosion.

'God Almighty! What was that?' he burst out. He broke into a run and as he reached the road he saw bright spouts of flame flare up from some twisted wreckage that lay a few hundred yards away. He raced towards it but was driven back by the heat and by further minor explosions that racked the already unrecognisable remains of the vehicle. A black pall of oily smoke wallowed above it.

Voices were calling from the village and he heard the sounds of cars being started. Footsteps rang out on the hard frosted surface of the roadway.

Dave stepped into the shadows.

John lifted his head from the patch of mud in which he lay. Something had happened but he was unable to focus his mind accurately. He struggled to his feet. He wiped the mud and dirt from his eyes and became aware of sounds coming from the bushes near the lake. A rustling of leaves and branches as if stirred by a mighty wind. He turned and saw a figure clad in white drift slowly through the trees, followed by a dark outline of great shapes. He blinked and they were gone. A moment later there came the sound of a great weight falling into deep water, but John heard nothing, for at that moment Sarah awoke.

'John!'

'Sarah! What's been happening?' I can't remember! Sarah! The last I knew was I rescued you from the lake!'

Sarah forced herself to sit up. Gradually her memory returned.

'I was in a terrible dream,' John was still speaking. 'It was so cold, and then I saw this girl!'

Sarah sat silent on the ground.

'And then I don't know what happened. In my dream everything suddenly faded .....'

'Did it really happen?' Sarah said, half to herself.

'I've just remembered,' said John, and there seemed to be new life in him as he spoke. 'We've got to get back to Dave Coulbeck. He's been waiting for us back along the track.

Simon went to warn him about a fallen tree-stump, while I came to look for you!'

Sarah glanced round and lifted herself wearily to her feet.

John grasped her arm.

'Judging by the way the land slopes towards the village if we head down this path we ought to reach the road that we were on when we saw the lake. If we can find the church we can make our way to the place where we left Dave.'

They staggered through the gate and along the lane. As they lurched past a row of cottages lights began to appear in the windows and doors began to open.

Sarah noticed that people were emerging from their houses all along the lane and heading in the same direction as themselves, pulling on overcoats and hats, some wearing nothing but night-clothes beneath.

Sarah and John began to pick up snippets of conversation as people rushed by. Luckily everyone was too busy to notice that they were soaked to their skins.

'Sounds like a car crash,' said John.

A feeling of apprehension flooded over him.

'I hope nothing's happened to Dave!'

Sarah grasped his arm firmly.

'It's not Dave,' she said softly.

They broke into a run, weaving and dodging between the small groups of people who were beginning to gather in the road.

As they reached the church they could see the glow of flames beyond the top of the hill. They hurried as fast as they could and were almost at the crest when the sound of a siren split the air. A police car swerved around the corner near the church and accelerated past the children, heading towards the flames.

By the time the children reached the wreckage a group of villagers were already gathered there.

'God help anyone who was in that!' commented a middle aged man clad only in pyjamas and overcoat.

'I was the first here,' added a small mousy woman who was shivering in the cold. 'No one could have got out. The heat was too bad!'

The two policemen were attempting to move the spectators to a safe distance from the burning wreck in case further explosions occurred.

'Don't suppose anyone saw it happen?' asked one of the policemen. There was a shaking of heads. 'I was the first here!' repeated the mousy woman proudly.

'I reckon whoever was in it was killed straight away! I never saw anyone get out. Burnt to a cinder if you ask me,' she added with relish.

The Land Rover still burned fiercely, casting shadows on the white paintwork of the police-car.

'Fire engine should be here anytime now,' muttered one of the policemen, 'though there's no call for the ambulance to break its neck getting here.'

Dave stepped back into the road and stood behind the increasing number of curious villagers.

'Always said there'd be an accident on this road sooner or later,' declared one of the locals. 'They come speeding through the village at all times of night!'

The surroundings changed to blue as flashing lights announced the arrival of the fire engine from Kineton. Quickly and skilfully they covered the wreck with chemical foam and within minutes the flames were smothered and the remains clicked and rattled in their death agony. The more morbid amongst the onlookers tried to peer into the crushed and twisted window frames, but the fires had done their work with ruthless efficiency and there was nothing for the untrained eye to see. People began to drift away, tut-tutting about the tragedy.

An ambulance struggled up the hill and veered across the road in order to back up to the wreckage. The police chatted briefly with the ambulance men, and stretchers and folded blankets were unloaded. The firemen packed away their extinguishers and began to attack the doors of the Land Rover with crow-bars. They were having little success, the metal was almost fused together and was still extremely hot to the touch.

'How many do you reckon are inside?' queried one of the ambulance men.

'Hard to tell,' replied the fireman who was working on the rear door. 'By my reckoning there's more than one or two. Funny how no one got out before the petrol tank went up. Still, that's the way it goes. If you're unlucky they can blow up before you have a chance to reach the door handle! Ah! That's it!'

There was a rasp of grinding metal and the rear hatch twisted away.

The policeman vomited at the smell of charred flesh.

'Dave!'

John and Sarah noticed him standing away from the crowd, obviously deep in thought. They rushed forward and he turned and caught them in his arms.

'Sarah! John! You're safe! What happened to you?'

'More to the point,' said John, 'what's been happening here?'

'Do you suppose it was Mother Shipton and her friends?' asked Dave slowly.

'I don't know how you'd ever tell for certain, looking at the state of that wreckage!' replied John.

'It *was* her!' Sarah's voice was emphatic. She gazed at the wreckage and at the stretchers covered entirely with blankets and containing very little bulk.

Sarah drifted away from them and made her way a little further up the hill.

'I felt so ill,' John said to Dave. 'I couldn't move or even speak! But I feel ever so much better now!'

Dave nodded.

'Simon was in the same state. I was trying to get to a telephone to call the police when I heard the crash.'

With a guilty start John realised that in the excitement of finding Dave again, he hadn't noticed that Simon was missing.

'Where's Simon now?' he asked anxiously.

'He's safe. I left him in the back seat of the Volkswagen. He's covered up in a blanket. If your recovery is anything to go by I should think he's on his feet again by now.'

They watched the doors of the ambulance slam shut. The driver climbed into the cab and it drove off slowly down the hill. The firemen were also preparing to leave and soon all that remained were the two policemen who were obtaining names and addresses from one or two of the villagers.

John grabbed Dave's arm.

'The treasure!'

In the excitement of the past half hour John had forgotten all about it.

'It'll be in the back of their truck!'

They began to stroll towards the wreckage. The back door had been twisted off by the firemen to enable the remains of the victims to be freed and John and Dave had no difficulty in peering inside.

A twisted mass of charred metal struts, iron pick-heads and shovels met their gaze.

Apart from that, nothing.

'Come on now sir,' one of the policemen was heading towards them. 'I'd keep well clear if I were you. It's not very pleasant in there.'

They moved back to where they had previously been standing.

'Sarah!' John called. She was near the hedgerow a little further up the road. Hearing John's voice she walked quickly back.

'It's not there,' he told her. 'The treasure wasn't in the truck!'

'I know,' said Sarah.

As they hurried back towards the track where the Volkswagen was parked, the police car started its engine and with a spurt of gravel it vanished into the dawn. They trudged on down the path, assailed by a strange feeling of anti-climax as reaction to their ordeal swept over them. It was a weary trio that arrived back at the place where they had abandoned the car but a few short hours ago.

'Where's Simon?'

A sense of foreboding crept over Sarah.

'If he's recovered he's probably gone looking for us,' said Dave reassuringly. 'Perhaps he's headed down towards the lake.'

They reached the Volkswagen door. In the back seat Simon lay stretched out. He was snoring gently.

Sarah began to laugh almost hysterically.

Dave unlocked the door and Simon sat up blinking his eyes.

'Where am I?' he croaked. He caught sight of John and Sarah.

'I had this dream about a girl ....' he began.

Twenty-One

Jack Parish hacked at the thickened stems of the hedgerow with a broad bladed axe. For the past two weeks he had been laying the hedges along the lane at the top of the village.

Every year he made the same pilgrimage to keep the boundaries of his land neat and tidy. He knew every inch of his hedges and often spoke to them as a father does to a wayward child, particularly when he discovered that they had grown too quickly and caused his craftsmanship to be hidden from view.

Not many people knew how to lay a hedge properly nowadays. It was a dying art.

He gathered an armful of branches together, and, kneeling down, started a little fire near the roadside. The twigs crackled and spat as the flames licked around them, invisible in the strong morning sunshine. He stood up and glanced incuriously at the break-down truck that was attempting to pull the burnt-out wreckage of a vehicle from the ditch a little further down the road.

Jack had noticed it earlier that morning when he had begun work. One or two of his acquaintances had passed the time of day by telling him of the accident the previous night. He shook his head sadly and returned to his task.

'Bloody hell! Just look at that!'

The driver of the breakdown truck wiped his blackened hands on his overalls and nodded to his mate who was getting out a thick tow-rope.

'It looks like it was hit by a bloody avalanche! How it got crushed like that is beyond me!'

He fastened the tow-rope around the burnt-out frame of the Land Rover.

'Must have rolled umpteen times to get that flattened,' his mate volunteered by way of explanation.

'Like it was hit by a bloody avalanche!' the driver repeated.

The powerful break-down truck yanked the wreckage from the ditch. The driver jumped down and loosened the tow-rope.

'What's this?'

His mate was turning the jib of the crane ready to lift the twisted mass of metal onto the truck.

Small chips of grey stone began to spatter onto the roadway from hundreds of creases in the metal that had been unfolded by the sudden tension of the tow-rope.

'Where the hell have all these bits of stone come from?' demanded the driver. He glanced into the ditch. There were no signs of any rocks there.

'It's like I said,' he asserted. 'It's been hit by a bloody avalanche.'

His mate joined him in the roadway.

'You don't get avalanches in this country,' he stated knowledgeably.

'I know that as well as you do, yer daft sod!' retorted the driver. 'Come on, let's get it loaded up. It'll be closing time and I'll miss me pint if we hang around much longer!'

Jack Parish watched as the truck rumbled by. The blackened shell of the Land Rover fastened on the back.

He turned to the hedgerow.

Ahead of him thrust the branches of an elder tree. 'I don't remember you, my friend,' he muttered.

He lifted his axe and slashed it to the ground.

27432783R00072

Printed in Great Britain
by Amazon